The *DOCTRINE*

of **RECOVERY**

A novel
by
MUTATIS MUTANDIS

eradicate poverty

remove the mask of racism

reverse climate change

hold politicians accountable

pay reparations

eradicate modern slavery

share corporate profits fairly

limit inherited wealth

restructure the delivery of aid

free refugees

abolish organized religions

validate equality for women

" *In 2024 the mysterious and elusive Herstel Fidia shakes up the world and sets humanity on a positive arc.*"

For
The quiet voices and transient souls.

The true measure of any society can be found in how it treats its most vulnerable members.

- Gandhi

PROLOGUE

The old man looked at the ocean as the sun set on the horizon. He looked at his great-grandson, who shared the balcony with him. The old man nodded slowly, indicating that bedtime was only a few minutes away.

"Papa, before I go, tell me again about the time long ago. The time long gone." The twelve-year-old stared at his grandfather intently. There was a hint of mischief embedded in the request, which they both recognized and acknowledged.

"Okay," agreed the old man. "Just a little bit. It was a long time ago, or so it seems."

They both made themselves comfortable, and the old man began reaching into the past. "How did it all start? Some say it began when a group of learned, religious men called Christians created a document which authorized them to control the exploration of the unknown world. Vast areas of Mighty Blue had not yet been discovered or visited by those who lived mainly in the northern part of the planet, and this document directed these men to claim all new land and resources for their king and country and for their decedents. They gave themselves this power in spite of the fact that there were people already living on the new lands. These people already living on the lands were not Christians—a religious group I'll explain later, as it's a very long story—but the visitors were, and the visitors felt that the Indigenous peoples who occupied the lands were inferior beings who should be subservient to the conquerors. Who should be ruled by them. So, the Indigenous people were trained to be Christians. Now, this doesn't seem right, but at the time the people from the north had skills and knowledge that made it possible for them to restrain and pacify the Indigenous peoples, and they also possessed better weapons, which allowed them to spread fear when needed. As a result, large numbers of Indigenous peoples were killed over the years of rule that followed. The lands were designated as colonies, and the management of those lands and its people was referred to as colonialism. During this period, the conquerors and their decedents grew wealthy and powerful. The new lands were stripped of their wealth, and the Indigenous peoples were subordinated and enslaved in a systematic fashion, which ensured that their status remained unchanged for hundreds of years. In short, the weak and disadvantaged remained so, and the rich and powerful grew even more so. But as time passed, those who suffered proved resilient and developed their skills and knowledge in their battle to survive making significant progress in the face of powerful obstacles. They wanted to be free of the shackles imposed on them by the conquerors and their ancestors. They prayed—there's that religious thing again—and fought hard. But they had hope, and many gave their lives to fulfil that hope.

"And then, in the year 2024—remember that the Doctrine of Discovery appeared in the fifteenth century, so many years had passed—the person you know as Herstel Fidia became known to the world and Mighty Blue went into a spin, shaking off the past and heading toward the period of peace and happiness in which we now live. It took a while, as humans have free will which they like to exercise, and not always with the best outcome, but here we are 2101, mostly concerned with creating a fruitful existence for everyone.

Tomorrow, I'll tell you about Herstel's first meaningful appearance in public and where he came from. Though not much of that is known. Mostly speculation. But in the grand scope of things, it's not especially relevant."

1

DESPERATE MEN DO DESPERATE THINGS

London, UK; February 2024
BBC TV Studios: Question Time -Live Broadcast

In a world of turmoil, a shining star appeared. Charismatic, cool and gentle were the reflections of his soul. His permanent smile engaged and disarmed everyone. Everyone.

"Are you happy?" he asked.

The people responded that they were.

"No, are you really happy?" he followed, ignoring their answer. "Empty your mind of needs. Drift, drift to the universe. It awaits you." His audience would listen and pause.

His first appearance - in the audience of a current affairs forum on live TV - stilled the room as he rose to his full six feet and spoke out of order and without invitation. He appeared to have a personal microphone which was patched into the studio's sound system. Long, tamed dreadlocks flowed over his shoulders, reaching well below his waist. He moved them aside with grace and ease. He smiled at nobody in particular. He focused on the cameras. Everyone stared at him. He was dressed in stylish African tribal designs. Pleasing to the eye.

"You know of all that is wrong. Of all that has been wrong. Of those who have been wronged. My work begins here, where so much was created to disable the human spirit. Soon, we will all only have long chopsticks. You will physically not be able to feed yourselves. You will have to feed others to create harmony and survive. Those who feel different will be rescued by the mushrooms. I urge you all to join me. Let us begin."

"Western culture is based on ideas of rugged individualism and competition. We think that survival of the fittest breeds competence and we ignore the pain and tragedy competition leaves in its wake. But if our species is to continue, if as individuals we are going to thrive, we must acknowledge how much we depend on one another and realize that mutual cooperation is essential. Ants and bees cooperate for the welfare of their entire anthill or hive. Surely, with our human intelligence, we can cooperate for the benefit of all."

He sat slowly. Smiling.

"Okay, thank you," responded the moderator who shuffled his notes impatiently and looked to his panelists for some kind of assistance. He'd lost his audience's attention.

Later, the figure of mystery engaged in conversation with several members of the audience who had followed him to a nearby café. Some observed quietly engulfed by a wave of expectation.

The production assistant, who the unsettled moderator tasked with investigating the surprise guest, offered her findings.

"He flew into London this morning from Madagascar. His name is Herstel Fidia. There were several Facebook posts of him at Heathrow. He attracted some attention. No records of him in Madagascar."

"Funny, if you Google his name, the word 'reparations' keeps popping up."

Immediately after the television appearance, small, intriguing adverts began appearing on traditional and social media platforms inviting people to visit mightyblue.com

Mighty Blue
You!
mightyblue.com

4

Hacker be true.

mightyblue.com

Little Johnny be you.

mightyblue.com

I am a Farmer of Abundance

mightyblue.com

Networker Networker!
Voulez vous couchez avec moi?

mightyblue.com

Balancers,
Stay humble
Work hard in silence.
Let success make the noise.

mightyblue.com

2

Monogram Coffee, Calgary, Alberta: February 2024

Each week, whenever their schedule permitted, two friends of some longevity met to discuss current affairs and offer solutions to the world's problems. Very rarely did they discuss their personal lives. They were middle class -"comfortable." Not sure about where they were in their lives, how they got there, and what the future held. The fires in their bellies had long since dimmed, and the pace of life was monotonous.

Alpha was obsessed with religion. He felt safe with the crutches it provided. He acknowledged the system had faults, but wondered, "How do you change it?"

"Let's talk endlessly," Alpha might've said, if he were being honest. Definitely no action. "You can't disturb my existence." Joyless, meaningless, insecure, he was looking for something - should be truth, but that's a tough call.

Beta was Zen. He understood that doing a little was enough. Especially a kind gesture. He understood the world was unfolding as it should. He enjoyed freedom of thought and expression. He had no fear of the consequences of change. He was happy to explore any avenue. He instilled fear and antagonism in Alpha, who needed to win all discussions and arguments. For Alpha, all conversation led to confrontation.

Alpha and Beta had independently stared at loneliness, despair, unhappiness, and frustration in different time frames of their lives—and they'd both found God staring back. They shared the same religion. Alpha had been weaned on it, as his family was part of a community-centered religion, which meant his entire life, bar regular education and employment, was immersed in community activities. Beta arrived later in life, and the community network and activities filled a void. They drifted together weekly at a cafe close to their offices, there to sort out the world's problems and express themselves. Alpha was doubly fortified by his religion and his life in academia as a professor at a local university. His faith revered educational achievements. Beta had concluded that academia was a form of religion. A hiding place for many. Members of their faith hung their hats on their qualifications. He was ambivalent. He wasn't impressed by money, power, or qualifications. He measured people by the personal qualities they displayed. Measured or valued, not judged. Most members of the faith were the opposite. They lauded wealth, position, and qualifications. Personal qualities, especially those demonstrably in conflict with the teachings of their faith, were secondary.

Alpha would take their weekly discussions—more akin to fencing—and mull them over day and night for the whole week. He liked to continue the thread, whereas Beta left the discussions in the café.

Beta: How are you doing?

Alpha: I'm great. How about you? I've been thinking about what you said last week. You may have something there. May is what I said. Hey, did you hear about some mysterious guy who interrupted Question Time- the BBC live discussion? I was watching it when that happened. Really weird. He kind of cut through everything like a hot knife through butter.

Beta: What did he say?

Alpha: Oh, in essence, we all know everything's not working, it all has to change, and now. And it's about to. It's almost like he's been listening to our conversations. I'm really looking forward to the Olympics. It's going to be a lot of fun. How about you? You think this Pope will resign too? He doesn't seem too committed. Did you see the ads for a site called Mighty Blue? They seem to be popping up everywhere.

Beta: Can't say I have, but you aren't the first person to ask. I'll see if I can spend some time on the whole thing. Has the feel of another bright, new shiny object. You know, like Bitcoin or AI.

Alpha: Just what we need.

Beta: I'm going to generalize here. You know I love to generalize. It's necessary to keep the conversation flowing.

Alpha: I know you do.

Beta: I think that our faith, as a microcosm of life, is in general quite racist in its regular day-to-day functions. In practice members look up to their white counterparts regardless of who they are and look down on the Blacks and Indigenous. It's a subtle, nuanced behaviour, always with a smile.

Alpha: You can't say that. It's not true.

Beta: It is. You're a perfect example.

Alpha: You really believe that ?

Beta: It's not a matter of belief. It's reality. And the Whites—you—conduct yourselves as superior and knowledgeable. If you can't live by the rules you profess to believe in and follow, it's a waste of time. So how do you deal with racism? You can't legislate it away.

Alpha: No, but with laws and good protection, you can isolate it, cage it, and remove its absolute power.

Beta: Ha Ha Ha! You can certainly talk about it. Let's see. We've been practicing racism unchecked for a few hundred years, so this will probably take several hundred years to get going.

Alpha: You disappoint me.

Beta: I disappoint me too. But I don't matter. You see that, lying there on the floor? That's my ego.

Alpha: This is another of your grey areas, like inequality. It's like the air we breathe. You can't just suck it out of the atmosphere. Everyone will eventually suffer.

Beta: The cost of inequality is in living. I can bathe you in statistics, but they can be meaningless. As Stalin said, "One death is a tragedy. One million deaths is a statistic." Inequality persists not by chance but by choice.

It causes direct harm to all of us. Governments can act. They can choose a violent, sexist, and racist economy or choose an economy in which nobody lives in poverty and neither does anyone live with unimaginable wealth, an economy in which people do more than just survive—they thrive. This is a generational choice. There is no shortage of money. Governments released sixteen trillion dollars to deal with the Covid pandemic. The poverty and LDC (Less Developed Countries) shortfall is far less than that. Twenty-six trillion dollars was spent on military last year.

Alpha: I have a question about inherited wealth. You want it all to stop. What about royalty?

Beta: Royalty? Easy. Wealth stays with the current holders with a very limited transfer to the next generation. And no annual maintenance payments. They work really hard, apparently. They should have no problem holding down a regular job.

Alpha: You do realize that the world is a complex place run by people in power. You have to accept that those in power are breathing a different oxygen, that they have a different vision and a more demanding set of needs than the average person. There's no seeing eye to eye. You're happy with a drip coffee, and I want a latte with cream. I don't really care what you need or are happy with. The important thing is I get what I want. What makes me happy. If I have to give up my latte so you can have half a cup of drip coffee, I'm going to think twice. I may do it once, but that's it. Is it the way we've been groomed, or is it human nature? You tell me.

Beta: Not this time, we need to go. What's the rest of your day like?

3

The Vatican was hosting its first consistory in nearly five years. The church had entered a watershed period and remained there. Its global presence was drifting. Its congregation glanced quickly and looked away. There were too many questions, and their need was now even greater than before.

He wasn't on the agenda, Herstel. In the halls of power—in every shape and form—he wasn't on any official agenda. He was spoken of a great deal, but nothing was said. Indeed, for this meeting, what was on the agenda and why? The Cardinal from Mali, the Archbishop of Bamako, not given to reticence, seized the opportunity during the informal session preceding the start of official business. He was still holding the Father's hand on greeting him and looked him straight in the eye.

"So Father, has news of the latter-day Robin Hood breached these walls? If so, what do you make of it?"

The Pope let go of the cardinal's hand and settled into the nearest chair, slowly and deliberately. This drew the attention of the entire room. With a wave of his hand, he spoke softly, gazing into a distance.

"He walks the Earth like lilies on a pond. He breathes air, and he is never there. He silences the voice of despair. The time has come for quiet meditation. The time has come for quiet voices. All must unite. All must bond. He's here to move the pieces into place. When he's done, he'll leave without a trace. This is the place for his heart. Everyone will know of his presence. Everyone will feel his love. There are those who will question. There are those who will fear.

When it's over, things will still be broken. But he will have put some pieces back in place. He floats on air. He's everywhere. He's in every heart. His is the love that binds. Everyone recognizes his part."

The archbishop recognized the very essence of Herstel, whom he had the pleasure of meeting several months before. Herstel, as is his wont, had shown up unannounced and uninvited.

"When did you meet?"

"We haven't. I know of him. Now let's get started, shall we?"

Unsettled and full of uncertainty, the cardinals slowly found their seats.

4

The survivor of every family who has innocently and involuntarily lost members from state-sponsored terrorism and war lives under a blanket of trauma. That damage moves from generation to generation. Who feeds the soul? How are they healed? What gives them release?

When Abdul, now the personal chef of the Russian president, was ten years old and living in Syria, he returned home from school to find that his entire family and their home had been evaporated by a Russian missile. The country's dictator had calculated it was in his interest to offer a helping hand to his Syrian counterpart. Birds of a feather plot together. Immediately after, Abdul also lost his country, as he was taken to Moscow by an NGO and placed with a family to be cared for. What is Abdul's therapy?

In Syria Abdul was considered bright and mature for his years; he sparkled yet had a calmness. The adults loved him. They felt settled in his presence and knew the children who gathered about him were safe.

"Abdul"! they would exclaim on seeing him. Not a greeting. Simply a statement for all in the vicinity. All was good.

On March 17, 2024, on a cold and grey Russian morning, a bus sped along the street in the village of Praskoveyevka with Abdul aboard half asleep, his head bouncing against the window. Images of his family filed past in his mind's window. He was neither asleep nor awake. He didn't know whether he was alive or dead. He was minutes away from serving the president his breakfast.

At the same time during a breakfast buffet at the United Nations Assembly in New York, the Russian delegation stuck together in silence. They were neither dead nor alive. The general consensus was that interest in the new speaker had temporarily removed them from centre of attention following their invasion of their neighbour. Or the centre of scorn, to be more accurate.

Neither Abdul nor the president greeted each other verbally nor visually as the former entered the breakfast room. As usual, the president was alone. Abdul had moved from the kitchen in a trance, having the retrieved the Glock—assembled the night before, complete with silencer. When Abdul pulled the trigger, the gun was only a few inches away from the back of the president's head. Simultaneously in New York, the head of the Russian delegation clumsily knocked a full bottle of Perrier off the table, and it shattered on the marble floor. All eyes on the ambassador. Soon all eyes on Russia.

Abdul removed his apron and made his way out of the building. Security were mildly surprised but uninterested. By the time he became of interest, Abdul had vanished. His life's purpose was over.

On the twentieth anniversary of the inauguration of the world's most powerful dictator, with no end in sight, he was found in his dining room, dead. Beside him was a white backpack containing a Glock 17 and a note: "No thought. No prayers. No meaningless words. A child is born and needs protection. Those who profit from harm will be rendered irrelevant. Anyone planning on repeating these unacceptable practices is advised to think again. You know who you are. So do we. We will be with you soon. Redemption, or flight?"

Chaos was expected on a national scale, as those next in the line of power entered in internal conflict with those who saw an opportunity for change.

The nation-state and patriotism increasingly seemed to serve little purpose in protecting the human rights of the people but were perfectly aligned with supporting exploitation by authoritarians and dictators. Given that you can fool all of the people some of the time and some of the people all of the time, there was enough ground to breed the exploiters who were leading millions of their supporters astray. Why the supporters disregarded their own interests could probably be explained as a lack of common sense. Everyone was hardwired with common sense. It was the divine gift for survival. However, if a person is unable to accept truth and reality, then the path forward is shrouded in a grey mist. It isn't possible for someone to engage in common sense if they were unable to accept truth and what was real. Without both elements in play, common sense was disabled.

The meticulous attention to detail of dictators in creating a protective network—survival was their primary concern—meant they were safe, and if they were challenged, it was usually by an ally who had plotted to rule within the existing status quo.

5

"To those in the part of the world known as Russia," said Herstel. "I say ignore the state and save the people." He was appearing at a Global Youth Conference in Haifa, Israel, focused on religious beliefs. His appearance was a surprise to the audience, and his introduction—by simple name only—didn't help alleviate the aura of mystery he'd created. In appearance, however - dressed in a spectacular robe of colorful Kenta cloth- he was hard to ignore. He agreed that the following tenets were a self-evident truths and ongoing aspirations: "Oneness of humanity, independent investigation of truth, peaceful consultation to resolve differences, gender equality, elimination of all forms of prejudice, abolition of extreme wealth and poverty, and world peace."

After a brief address, Herstel urged his audience to suspend discussion and to meditate and listen to the silence. "Fewer questions," he said. "because we already know the answers." As he slipped away from the crowd, and there was, of course, the inevitable question: "Who was that?"

"Be prepared to take up the reins at all levels," Herstel later said, staring into the camera at Tel Aviv airport in answer to the question from the news crew who demanded to know who he was, what he had to say and what message he had for their viewers.

What followed globally was anxious expectation, not chaos. Anxiety was replaced by a calmness. The world was unfolding the way it should.

Following the Russian incident, the popular press, in need of further drama, created a mythical group they dubbed The Backpackers to whom they attributed responsibility for the assassination. This idea generated a great deal of excitement, not least in the endless speculation of their next target.

In truth, such a group did exist. Created by a legendary soldier who'd fought for several armies and was considered the elite of the elite – the quintessential warrior. Increasingly, he felt something approaching guilt and remorse for his actions: a long life of executing the orders of his political superiors. He was single-minded and focused, as they undoubtedly were. He was instinctively driven by survival. It was his driving force.

Yet, why did he execute their plans? He was empathetic and cared for human life, yet his entire training and purpose was to extinguish some lives to protect others. It didn't make sense. He had battled with this conundrum for a few years growing, increasingly unsettled.

Now he faced an impasse. He called on his training. Keep it simple and uncomplicated.

If his life was to be dedicated to the preservation of life, then there was a need to terminate those whose actions and aims were to subjugate and eliminate others with little regard to life.

The net result would be a hired gun fighting for human life. Save as many as possible. Determine where the most effective blows were to be struck. Do so in stealth. Like a thief in the night, provide no target for retaliation but encourage those who created and supported the targets to reconsider their journey and actions. He created a group of similar minded individuals. Members didn't know each other; they only knew and communicated with the leader. They were anonymous, as were their locations.

The United States claimed to have kept the peace for over 75 years. Said Nietzsche, "All things are subject to interpretation. Whichever interpretation prevails at a given time is a function of power and not truth." During that period, millions of lives were sacrificed or lost by political decisions made in the pursuit of corporate and national power.

The purpose of the state was to protect individual human rights, yet in most cases the individual was a victim of the state - at the mercy of its faceless power.

There was no legal or illegal accountability for erroneous behaviour in power. Leaders protected each other no matter how terrible their crimes. And no leaders left office with impecuniosity.

The warrior concluded: "I will change the status quo. I will create a group of like-minded self-sacrificing individuals - the people's Samurai - and like thieves in the night remove those broken obstacles to the safety of humanity. I will also remove those who are in waiting to fill the void and perpetuate the status quo. We will be hermits. Unknown to each other but with a common cause. We will exist in the shadow. We will be untraceable. But the world will feel our presence."

The Backpackers lived by the Bushido code of righteousness, loyalty, honour, respect, honesty, courage, and consistency, and each had a Bushido tattoo for identification should it be necessary in cases of dire emergency. Most importantly, those who aspired to use the channels of higher office entrusted in them by the plebian majority would be made aware that the rules of operation had to be rewritten.

Musashihe adopted the name of Japan's most famous warrior as a reminder of his duty—stood boldly upright and breathed deeply. There was clarity in his mind. He'd arrived at his purpose.

He had to begin his mission without delay.

6

Associated Press, Moscow: March 24, 2024

The President of the Soviet Union is dead. It is reported he was found this morning in his private quarters. Further reports are emerging that he was found alone, and the cause of his death is unknown. His personal chef, who is normally in attendance at this time, has been reported missing.

The people of the Soviet Union, as elsewhere, are in shock.

What followed was the battle of the deputies and the battle of the civilian administrators and the military. A non-political body of citizens emerged as the management group led by experienced civil servants and experts in every relevant field. Leadership by consensus. Welfare of the people, not the state.

7

On April 21, 2024, thousands of runners and spectators gathered in the centre of London for one of the city's most exciting annual events. Goodwill, happiness, and positive energy ruled the day.

Wearing the black Magali's sports vest of Madagascar, Herstel moved among the elite athletes, nodding and making friendly gestures. There were 50,000 runners participating in the marathon, but just forty elite athletes competed in the professional race. Herstel was a new face in this group which moved almost with unchanged membership through the six major marathons in the world. He qualified from Madagascar and re-inforced his time in the Nigerian marathon. He was the oldest of the group. Fifty years old but seeming not a day over thirty, he drew little attention from his contenders, all of whom were concentrating on themselves. The media focused on the known names.

With its extensive global TV coverage, the event offered Herstel the opportunity to address items on his Doctrine of Recovery, which would begin the transformation of the lives of a significant portion of the world's population. The financial consequences would create the first crack in the existing global financial system

When Herstel broke from the leading pack thirty kilometres out as they emerged from the underpass in Blackfriars proceeding along the Thames Embankment, the sports journalists scrambled for information about him as the break was significant: he ran the second half of the marathon in the fastest time recorded, breaking the record set in 2022. Drawing all attention, this lone, elegant figure smoothly sailed along parallel to St James Park and onto the mall in the London sunshine, approaching the tape in front of Buckingham Palace, his smile and flowing dreadlocks underlined an effortless run. Herstel was pleased with his execution and eagerly anticipated the post-race press conference, which was his main goal.

The sports journalists, realizing they were witnessing an important moment, reached out to share with their mainstream news colleagues, those from the cable networks who worked hard at creating tantalizing news headlines such as:

See what this celebrity has for dinner!
You will never believe this!
If only you could see this.
Congressman accused of . . .
Mystery runner overwhelms field in London marathon.
Were drugs a factor in marathon win?

Herstel choose the event to announce his poverty initiative—the first item on the Doctrine of Recovery—and draw awareness of mightyblue.com an all-encompassing resource website, which offered support to everyone. The cable networks switched gears when news of the mystery runner broke. The poverty initiative caught everyone off balance. The sporting fraternity felt invaded and were irritated that their event had been hijacked.

To add to their dismay, when the current affairs journalists showed up-after he had addressed the crowd - Herstel had already vanished. Frantic investigation aided by the little information available on his entry application only led them collectively to a dead end. Others decided to look into the validity of the initiative Herstel described. Mighty Blue was investigated by the media. Many paused to ponder the possibilities and consequences of the actions and ideas described on Mighty Blue and Herstel had replaced the America president as the top global news item on all search engines and social media.

Herstel waited until all the questions that rained down on him petered out. He didn't answer any but signaled with a raised palm that he was ready to speak.

"I ran for Mighty Blue.

I ran for the future of humanity.

I ran well within my capabilities, but that is of little importance.

You must now all reimagine yourselves and run for your future.

Mighty Blue will provide all you need for your journey.

On May 15 - the International Day of Families - the stain of poverty will begin to be erased. On that day, what are you planning to do? For yourself? For your friends and family?

On that day, all those who are currently suffering from poverty will begin to experience change in their lives.

Nine percent of the world's population - 800 million exists on less than $2.15 per day. Now remember this moment because wherever you are, whoever you are, you can be part of the change. Visit Mighty Blue and reimagine yourself.

So how will we disable poverty?

There are enough supplies of food and materials in the world to feed and shelter everyone. It's just that the impoverished cannot afford to access them because of lack of finance.

On this day, all those under the umbrella of poverty around the world will receive a phone followed by transfer of funds to enable them to buy food and materials to meet their basic needs. Funds will be in the form of digital currency, and those who receive them will be able to perform regular banking activities via Mighty Blue's bank.

Supplies of food and materials will be put in place by most of the existing government and charitable organizations. They will simply operate in a more efficient manner to benefit those in need, as was their original mandate.

This will happen because those of you who work for those organizations will transform them and yourselves. Any help you require to initiate and sustain you on your new journey you will find through Mighty Blue. Thousands of companies around the world will provide a supply chain. The initial funds and all subsequent transactions will be in digital currency underwritten by Mighty Blue financial.

> *We're going to shake up the world*
> *You are going to shake up the world.*
> *Be the change you want to be.*
> *Be the change you want to see."*

Herstel paused and surveyed the crowd who were subdued and puzzled. A few questions were asked, mostly about Herstel, not about his message. The sports reporters were amused. Another sports personality seeking attention.

And who or what is Mighty Blue was the question most listeners would soon be seeking answers to. The answer was a humane future. Visitors would find answers to all of their question, and much more information imbedded in the website. The ambassador of Mighty Blue proposed what he described as inevitable. Mighty Blue was a resource portal that offered everyone the opportunity to reimagine themselves and participate in setting humanity on a sustainable course.

Seventy-three per cent of the work force was stressed out by financial worries.

Work had to become a service for humanity, not for profit. AI robotics would replace manual and technical tasks. Work related to service would be financially rewarded, and AI would initially be managed by the Mighty Blue Network.

Mighty Blue's advanced software would identify and verify obstacles. It would determine solutions and provide resources as needed, material or human. Income distribution would be based on social and political parameters, and data was subject to review and change.

Buddhism taught that joy and happiness arise from letting go. Herstel asked people to please take an inventory of their lives. There were things they'd been hanging on to that really weren't useful and instead actually deprived them of their freedom.

"Find the courage to let them go," said Thich Nhat Hanh, the Buddhist monk known as the father of mindfulness.

"Reimagine your life with Mighty Blue," said Herstel. "Breath and immerse yourself. What would you like to change about your life that will bring you happiness, fulfillment, and peace? What are the obstacles preventing you from achieving what you want and need? Identify them, and Mighty Blue will assist in removing some or all of them and allow you to continue on a more rewarding journey. This is your opportunity to improve your life as you see fit. Seize the day!"

Visitors to Mighty Blue registered and began an interactive journey assisting them to take more control of their lives and contribute constructively to facilitate change where ever necessary.

Registering with Mighty Blue required the following information:

- Name and address
- Job and profession
- Volunteer interest
- Recreation interests
- Financial overview
- Needs
- Challenges
- Career
- Goals
- Education
- The contact information of friends, family, and community members who could benefit from reimagining themselves.

Registration was followed by simple positive suggestions:

Be your own gatekeeper.
Organize your own labour.
Be your own union.

Be productive.
Be useful
Be the change you want to see.
Blue will support you.
Be bold.
Be fearless.
What do we know of what we know?
It all changes with the tide.
What looks better? High or low tide?
We don't know until we take time to look.
And then we move on.
Life should not be a battle.
It's a journey.
Make yours a calm and peaceful one.

Herstel concluded calmly but with passion:

These are the thoughts which should prevail to guide you forward: "I've lived this life with the curtains drawn. Let it all go on. Don't involve me. Now the curtains gone, and the house is demolished. It's me. I wasn't paying attention. I am now. It's time for a turnover. It's serious. We're all players. No more sitting on the sidelines.

I choose
to live by choice, not chance;
to be motivated, not manipulated;
to be useful, not used;
to make changes, not excuses;
to excel, not compete.
I choose self-esteem, not self-pity.
I choose to listen to my inner voice,
not to the random opinions of others.
Our motto is Be Kind.

Everyone has the right to satisfy their basic needs of food, water, air, clothing, and shelter.

If we mobilize the human desire to matter and be safe, we can assist each other to at least satisfy basic needs. We have the resources globally to meet the basic needs of everyone on this planet – Blue.

Currently an inequitable system creates poverty, hunger, strife, and civil unrest.

These changes will set a course of transformation to benefit all.

They require the investment of everyone, individually or as a group, to ensure implementation and change.

Be brave. These changes are inevitable.

Do not procrastinate. Help yourself. Help others.

All the resources you need are available at mightyblue.com.

Reimagine yourself and get started.

And what are these changes you wonder? What are they indeed?

You know what they are. You've known for hundreds of years. I will simply remind you.

We're setting the course of recovery. Choose your area of activity. Others will lift the torch elsewhere. Engage your friends and family and community.

Currently over one billion people live on less than one dollar a day. Our goal is to provide them with at least four dollars per day initially. Equally important, they will have secure access to those funds. We will begin to lift everyone—developed and LDC- out of the jaws of poverty in the immediate future. And by immediate, I mean now. The process has begun.

Millions everywhere, as we speak are being given phones, smart phones, funds to enable them to purchase food, materials to build shelter, medicine, clean water, and the tools to create and improve their future.

These elements of development and help go directly to those in need. There is no third-party distribution to recipients.

If you're involved in the huge diaspora of profit-making activities known as aid, your assistance and expertise through your current position will allow you to participate in this process through Mighty Blue. You must switch to service non-profit. If the current system presents you with roadblocks, Mighty

Blue will remove them so you can concentrate on achieving what is necessary and important.

And so it will be in every walk of life.

Examine what you do. What are your goals and plans? What are the obstacles in your way? Reimagine yourself and begin to live. The arc of human existence is now moving upward.

8

Associated Press, Beijing: April 24th, 2024

In an official statement, the Chinese Communist Party has confirmed the death of its leader, the president of China. The cause of death is unknown at present. There are unconfirmed reports that a white backpack was found at the scene of death containing two notes: one was the Universal Declaration of Human Rights, the other a handwritten note: "There is no hiding place for those who choose to be enemies of humanity. They will be culled from the herd."

It is expected that a new leader will be announced within days. Leaders around the world have expressed their sympathy and shock. The whole of China is in a state of mourning.

9

Beta: Hey! How's it going?

Alpha: Oh, pretty good. What's new?

Beta: So this Mighty Blue is interesting. I've spent so much time on it. Looks like it's some kind of portal. There are some weird things about it. It's vastly complicated, and at the same time, simple. Can't figure out who's behind it and what they're doing. Profit or non-profit? Info site or commercial?

Alpha: Come on, you're the technical wizard. What is it offering?

Beta: Still trying to work that out in my head. It does seem wild. Here goes. The concept: The world as we know it is full of problems. Some would appear existential. The reasons are apparent to anyone with an ounce of intelligence or who is reasonably informed. We human beings have the ingenuity and resources to change the world's course to make it better. We as individuals need to change our thinking, our behaviours, our lives, our intent to survive

There's a myriad of obstacles preventing us from doing so. We can go to Mighty Blue and identify ourselves, our challenges and goals, and then set about overcoming the obstacles and achieving our goals. And then, wait for it, Mighty Blue will somehow provide us with all of the resources you need to make the change. I mean resources as in all aspects of your life: work, home, community, friends, finances etc. Yes, I know it's complicated.

Alpha: So how long has it been around? Is it operational? How does it work? Sounds like a cult scenario.

Beta: Don't know how long it's been around. The back end is obscure, but it's functional. You register and reimagine yourself along the guidelines I mentioned, and then you set about living your life the way you wish. If you hit any obstacles, Blue will help you deal with them. You just throw off the shackles. Oh, and you know that info we talked about last time? You were supposed to figure out the math about inequality and poverty. It's on the site in a section called Blue Notes.

Not only that, but there are lots of other ads on the Internet—and the regular media that lead to various sections and groups on Mighty Blue. These are groups you can join to help the cause. You can also invite your friends and community members to join and help themselves.

Did you say cult-like?

Alpha: What do they do? And who is in charge of it all?

Beta: There are no evident leaders or leader as such. But all research references lead to that mysterious guy you saw on TV—Herstel Fidia—and there's no real information on him.

However there are several identified groups that are interesting:

The Bushido: Only for those with a samurai in their soul. That's all there is here. Weird.

The Shadow: Those in positions of immense power, be it financial or otherwise.

The Balancers: Fairness, justice and objectivity are the central elements required.

The Hackers: Supreme IT skills get you through the door.

The Farmers of Abundance: Global organizers and administrators.

The Johnnies: Practical and hands-on.

The Resistors: Those who are drawn to the negative and are led by ego finding solace in groups who are afraid to scratch the status quo, subconsciously existing in fear, paying little heed to truth and common sense.

Not sure why they would invite those not on board to participate.

Alpha: And what do you do with the crazy people? Sorry, I mean those with mental health issues. And what about all those who feel they're losing their power and position? Are they able to use the Mighty Blue resources to cement their position and security? There's going to be huge conflict. Humanity isn't a simple creature.

Beta: Ah! Blue acknowledges that. It says, that as history demonstrates, it is in the flawed nature of human beings to pursue confrontation and to be driven by ego. But with these changes - the Doctrine of Recovery - I didn't mention that did I? - humanity will be on a more positive and fruitful course with more people benefitting from what we have. It will not be utopia, but it will be better than what we have now. Those who wish to follow opposite routes are free to do so. Birds of a feather will flock together. Blue encourages us all to do what we can to ensure those flocks have the resources to exist in harmony. Needs, hunger, and fear generate conflict, as we know.

However, there will be less conflict. The Doctrine of Recovery will appear challenging, but it will assist hugely. It's the path forward. It's written, says Herstel.

Alpha: What is it?

Beta: It's a summary of the problems humanity faces and the solutions. There are no full details until September, when it will all be revealed. Sounds biblical, doesn't it? I guess Herstel will appear on a mountain top soon, unannounced as usual, and boom!

Alpha: Quite some achievement even for the "viral" environment in which we live. He only appeared about ten weeks ago, and he's now the planet's main event, in spite of the fact that we know nothing of him. Apparently, all roads lead to a dead end as far as his history and background are concerned.

Beta: Oh, that reminds me. There's a statement on the website that says—and I'll just summarize—the operating system and software used by Mighty Blue, and by default its registrants and group members, are virtually impregnable. Meaning that all of their activities have no barriers and they themselves are not hackable.

Alpha: Is that possible?
Beta: Not in the world we're familiar with.
Alpha: All right. See you next week?

10

The members on the production team of Britain's most hard hitting and serious current affairs interviews had been together for quite a few years. They exuded an air of familiarity and weariness. The global news landscape had been lettered with calamity, and it was increasingly difficult to find people in positions of power willing to submit themselves to scrutiny. The presenter, Robert Ramjohn, was still fresh and committed to his craft after seven years of interviews, most of which had evolved into confrontations. He was a man with a hammer, and he was always looking for a nail. He was fresh but bored. He reviewed the rollcall of this week's second-tier politicians, corporate leaders and various entertainers for the next ten days. They were all in need. He wasn't.

"Okay," boomed Robert, drawing everyone's attention. "I've reviewed the bios and social corporate CVs. Is there anything off the beaten track you'd like to throw my way?"

He scanned the group and their silent responses via shaking heads.

"You have to admit, it's a lame lineup." This signalled the end of the meeting, and they all rose to their feet, gathering their numerous technology devices.

"Maybe we should have said yes to Herstel," Adam said aloud to no one in particular. Adam Sector, an intern, had joined the group four weeks earlier straight out of university and was now quite disillusioned about this dull future his chosen field was revealing. He had imagined fast-paced, exciting verbal interaction and physical movement, as witnessed on his TV screen.

"What?" Ramjohn's deep baritone, dripping with drama, filled the room.

Everyone stopped and gazed at Adam. He gazed back, having forgotten what he had said.

"Who are you, and what did you say?" inquired Robert.

"I don't know if you've heard of him, but someone who has recently been on the news called and requested to be on the program. Next week. He was specific about the date. 'Inflexible,' he said. I explained the booking process, which meant there was no chance of his being on the program, and I thanked him for his interest."

"Did you know about this?" Robert inquired of the senior producer, who nodded affirmatively. "Do you know who Herstel Fidia is?" Robert was now Shakespearian in his delivery. He was alive again. For the past several weeks he had been following the trajectory of Herstel's public appearances, trying to make something of it. He sensed the man was heralding some important changes, or rather, he hoped as much. He had a myriad of questions for Herstel, who seemingly had no answers, avoided giving any clues to who he was or what he was about, and simply announced events and activities that were to take place in the future. How and by what means, he wouldn't delve into.

This was Roberts dream come true. "Clear the schedule of these dingbats and book Herstel. I will do my own preparation for this. Let me know as soon as he's confirmed."

11

H erstel had declined to meet Robert informally just prior to the interview.

As the clock approached the hour of broadcast, Robert was almost hyperventilating. The importance of the pre-interview meeting, an automatic feature not given much thought, dawned on him. Here he would quickly assess his victim and establish who's boss. Now he felt vulnerable, he was on the back foot.

Robert proceeded to his chair and sat across the table from the calm, motionless figure who engaged him with unrelenting eye contact. He was a little overwhelmed by Herstel's physical appearance. In dress, he was spectacular, reminding Robert of the Malian musician Habib Koite, who he had interviewed a few years back and who also adorned himself in glorious African designs.

Caught unawares Robert was tense. The tension was released when Herstel revealed a sparkling set of ivories and a wink of his eye.

Floor manager: "We are live in five, four, three, two, one."

Robert sat up and was quick to load and fire.

Robert: Herstel Fidia, welcome. I must say this is an unusual situation. Normally, prior to this moment, I would share with our viewers a brief bio of our guest. But in your case, you have provided no information. Also, our guests are typically invited to participate after due diligence and scrutiny, but you contacted our production staff and requested to appear on this specific date.

So, as you would imagine, I have numerous questions. Why don't you tell me who you are, who you represent, what your mission is - as you are clearly on a mission - and what we can expect from you in the immediate future.

Herstel: Thank you, Robert. It's my pleasure to be here. I'm sure time is of the essence. I don't want to disrespect you, but why don't we start with your latter questions, and we can return to me later.

Robert: All right, then, here are some of the things you've said. Poverty and hunger in the world as we know it will be eradicated shortly. This will be facilitated by the supply of phones and funds to those in need. The global aid system will be hijacked in its present form and utilized to assist with the process. Any individual can, with the help of the Mighty Blue portal, reimagine themselves and create the life they desire relieved of financial pressure or peer pressure. Why would this happen? How will it happen?

Herstel: Robert we all need answers in this time of change. You more than most, having interviewed VIPs for years, know that truth and fabrication is a heady mix that chills the senses and disables the limbs. Day after day, we – humanity - do the dance in spite of the fact that the majority want and need a change of the tune.

Let us begin with the facts (calmly smiling): Set aside gender inequality, financial inequality, racism, classism, greed, physical and mental handicaps, environmental challenges, and numerous other petty obstacles that humans are prone to treat as important. Rath look at what we have. We have: one planet, eight billion people, a net abundance of resources, ingenuity, resilience, a common desire for basic human needs, no idea of the purpose of existence, a universal understanding of the intangible element we know as love, and a basic desire to be happy.

What makes us happy and how we achieve happiness are complicated ideas, but seemingly we feel we can achieve happiness at the expense of the happiness of others. This Robert is patently stupid.

So, let's look at dealing with the basics. Supply everyone with basic human needs. Then we can begin, as a collective, to move toward a level of individual happiness. There are, of course, those whose knee-jerk reaction would be, 'Hey, that's not possible without me suffering in some way.' They're probably right. But so be it. How do we proceed? And how? What needs to be done? We, as a collective, need to implement and execute all elements of the Doctrine of Recovery. I've just mentioned only a few. The full list will be revealed in September at the United Nations General Assembly.

The future is written, Robert. Humanity and the planet will survive and prosper. Of course, there are those who will try to plot a different course. We are humans after all, and we have free will. But there is destiny. So to those people, I say don't stand in the hallways. Don't block up the halls. To all others, we soar like eagles. This, Robert, is what is beginning to happen. Humanity is going to dance to a different tune.

We talk arrogantly about saving the planet. The planet isn't in danger. Nature has its own checks and balances. Its humanity playing the survival game. With the changes I propose we will turn the clock back on the decay of the environment. Earth will be blue again. Mighty Blue. Herstel paused to smile. We have a planet, Robert. We are one people. But here are some questions to ponder. Who are we, us humans? What have we done so far? What are we capable of in the future? Where is the enemy we all constantly live our lives in fear of? Our enemy is not other people. As Thich Nhat Hanh said, our enemy is hatred, violence, discrimination, and fear.

Now, Robert, if I could flip a switch and ask you to reprogram your social, work, recreation routines and goals to make happiness the motivating factor, would you be able to create a new program? Life, I'm sure, is not a bed of roses. Even if it was, that would still be uncomfortable. Herstel laughs.

Robert is caught off guard. He's supposed to be the interviewer. This is becoming personal. He needs a question that will allow him to bypass the question and get back on track.

Robert: How are we meant to believe or even understand all these things you say will occur? It's a big ask.

Herstel: You want proof instantly. Would it be easier if I presented this as a modern-day Christian? There are many things you will not understand, many that make no sense, and many that defy logic and reality. But I ask you to have faith. Have faith and believe, and your life will be better either in this world or the next. Now, Robert, is that easier for you?

Robert: Well, hardly.

Herstel: Why not? It's the status quo in which you exist and in which humans have existed for hundreds of years. Herstel smiles benevolently. We're getting off track. Every individual has an innate desire to live freely in comfort, safety, and good health. That's why we work. We're not all equal in so far as we all have different skill sets, which, depending on our time in history, will bring rewards to some of us. Those with other skill sets that are not valued at that time, are left to toil. In a sharing environment where we help each other, the number of disadvantaged decreases.

To date, the great progress we've made is recognizing the qualities we should adopt and celebrate to make life liveable for the majority of us.

Those qualities, for the large part, were imbedded in religious texts, but the religious leaders perfected a system that was based on hierarchy, opposed to common sense and humane teaching and exploited the weak.

The rich and powerful did the same.

The average person pursuing these desirable goals lives in fear.

So here we are, the majority living in fear and need, while the rich and powerful, who make the rules that do not apply to them, grow stronger and impregnable in their material wealth.

Those who live in fear conceal their principles and ethics to protect themselves and their family and friends. This is the current rule of survival: individual versus individual, group versus group, countries versus countries.

Greed and instant gratification are the guiding lights.

How can we change this course? In real terms, where does the power lie? Let's look at poverty, aid, wealth, racism, politics and religion. These are only a few of areas which need rewriting.

Robert, you of all people know the answers to fix the broken systems. But you won't venture there because it's all impossible. Or so you believe.

Don't underestimate the ingenuity and resilience of the human creature. Humans only real fear are themselves. We are all capable of infinite good and infinite evil. Pursuing the former and keeping the latter in check is the trick.

And on this journey, we need to help ourselves first and then others.

We know there's enough food in the world to feed everyone adequately. There are enough material goods to provide everyone with basic comforts. So why are there 800 million people living in poverty? Because they simply do not have the funds to purchase food and material goods to satisfy their basic needs. Yet there's enough dormant wealth available to bridge that gap. We're going to use that wealth - wherever we find it - to bridge that gap. This process has begun. Soon, its effect will become apparent.

The developed world has a vast amount of debt. The least developed countries have considerably less debt. If we were to equal the playing field, poverty in the least developed countries would be alleviated. Of course, that debt in the developed world is largely used to purchase goods and food that is produced in the poorest countries. The irony is that most of that food is being wasted or misused by the developed world, leading to health problems. What will these practices lead to if they continue? What will be our destiny if we blindly continue on the present path?

Consider this, Robert, what is destiny, and what is free will? We have free will. We need to make use of it individually and collectively.

A large amount of accumulated wealth in the world resulted from illegal and inhumane exploitation of the masses and disadvantaged, both in the pre- and post-industrial times and currently by corporations, the royal families and landed gentry of today.

Robert, wrong is wrong, and right is right! The hoe and lathes have been replaced by the keyboard and warehouses, but the hierarchy of power remains the same.

Accumulated wealth moves through generations without accountability.

Inherited wealth should be identified by its source and redistributed to those who contributed to its creation unwillingly and illegally.

The current wealth being created should be limited in terms of what it can offer to inheritance on a private level. Rather, those who are contributors to its creation at every level should be rewarded fairly from the chief executive to the labourer and delivery person. They all matter. Everyone should share in the net profits of a commercial venture.

We internalize fear. It's apparently linked to survival. It's also linked to tribalism and nationalism and any other grouping you can imagine. If we begin to think, identify, and repair our own shortcomings, we will throw off the shackles that force us to elevate our own net worth by stepping on others. We can then start to build our worth and esteem by helping others.

But first we must examine ourselves, truthfully, and value those against whom we are prone to be prejudiced. It's a necessary therapeutic path. It will not be easy, and it will not happen overnight. But once we recognize the path, we can step onto it and persuade others to follow us by example. Individually, we can be shining lights.

Robert, we are all of equal worth, but we are all different. That should be something we celebrate. Our diversity's a joy. Using diversity of any form for negative purposes is just weakness and stupidity.

There is one profession that remains unaccountable. It attracts those who seek power, which is an oxymoron when you acknowledge its purpose is to serve others. Politicians. Every other professional is punished if there is dereliction of duty, acts of ill intent or negligence or criminality. Yet politicians document their intent and promises, are elected as a result, and remain unpunished when they fail to act as promised or where they deliberately act against the wishes or welfare of the people they serve. It isn't voluntary work. They should be prosecuted. We should begin this process now by requiring current incumbents twelve months to enact the promises they made in the past thirty-six months or resign.

All new aspirers to office will be playing by different rules.

Aid! What is this? How does this work now, and who benefits? The same can be said of religion. Let's deal with aid firstly. Government aid: how much is donated annually, how much is used for purchase of military and administration, how much gets to those in need.?

Non-governmental aid: similar analysis. If you examine these numbers, they exemplify the misuse of power and wealth.

The current channels of distribution should be dismantled and legitimized. I think in a fairer world, you'll see less wrongdoing. But we, as humans, have a predilection for the other side of the track. That's okay. Once we're all aware it's not utopia, those who engage in malpractice will be dealt with accordingly.

And finally, religion. Do you have the time?

Current religious practices subject vast numbers of people to servility and fear, elevating some members to positions of enormous power. Religions accumulate and horde great wealth, which the mostly disadvantaged congregations can ill afford.

What's the net gain from religion? It has to be firmly in the negative column. We need to stand on our own two feet and help each other. Organized religion isn't only a crutch but a burden to the individual who doesn't realize it. Fear is seen as faith. Spirituality is the natural path. There's no religion in spirituality, but there's embedded in religion an element of spirituality. Pursuit of spirituality empowers and frees the individual.

Therefore all benefits and social and financial advantages enjoyed by the religious organization should cease immediately.

All accumulated wealth should be identified by a third party and distributed to the local congregations. Free the people, Robert !! Initially, they will be fearful, but thereafter, joyful.

Robert: What you're describing is best labelled as utopia. And I put it to you, sir, that expecting any small part of this—needless to say all of it—to come to fruition betrays a great degree of naivety and very little understanding of how the world works and why it does.

How is any of this going to happen?

And who are the players in what would entail a truly global operation in terms of resources wealth and personnel?

Herstel: It's happening as we speak. It has begun. The Mighty Blue, as we refer to the Earth, has begun to turn on a positive axis. There are various groups at work - that have been at work for some time - enabling the implementation of some of what I've described.

For example, the United Nations and the aid network, both government and civilian, have created over time the bureaucratic machinery to deliver the goods required to alleviate poverty. We will use the existing channels, with a few adjustments to assist with delivery.

Those who work for these organizations are aware of their failings. They can individually step up and make their positions positive and useful. Any fear they have of contradicting their supervisors, of personal, financial and career detriment, will be taken care of by the Mighty Blue resources, allowing them to get on with the work at hand. This will free them to function with purpose and without any pressure from their personal needs.

Robert, the United Nation's list of social development goals, which they plan to achieve by 2030, has some threads in common with the Doctrine of Recovery.

I will elaborate on the Doctrine, but I guess your immediate reaction would be to ask me how I'm going to achieve this. Yet I wonder if you were interviewing someone from the United Nations about its goals whether you'd ask specifically how they'd achieve them.

Let's examine the purpose of life! The universe, nature, good and evil are all more powerful and complex than can be encompassed by the concept of an ever-watchful deity who will, on request, sanction acts with benevolence.

The fabric of existence—pre-birth, life, and post-death—is far more complicated and beautiful, an infinite flow of positive and negative energy that somehow influences and impacts life on earth and beyond. This short time on Mighty Blue is indeed fleeting. Can we agree that human beings inherently are good and if their needs are met, left to their own devices, will gravitate to a peaceful existence seeking happiness. This is how it ideally should be.

But alas, there's another side to humans. One attracted to power and greed. Those who operate from this place instill fear and servility in others. On a grand scale they disregard the natural desire for good, and prey on the less fortunate who are always on a course of struggle.

The loud and aggressive minority control the quiet and peaceful.

Everyone is involved as we speak, Robert. From the arborist in British Columbia to the politician in Washington. The philanthropist in need to share, to the billionaire on his last lap who maybe views his existence from a lens of futility.

Millions are getting on board within their existing parameters at home and at work. They are quietly putting matters on an even keel. The change is rising like the flood waters created by a tsunami crashing ashore. Soon everyone everywhere will be affected.

We have the ears of many in power, we have the attention of those invisible hands that guide the future. We have the ears of many who want to contribute to positive change. Mighty Blue is offering them the opportunity to do so significantly.

Where is MLK?

Where is Gandhi?

Who else is there?

Where are the purveyors of good, without gain?

They were paid lip service, and then we wallowed in their quotes, which adorn yoga studios everywhere. They were given only so much leeway until they appeared to be a threat to the status quo. To no effect.

Why repeat the words if you don't listen and act?

"Lest we forget." Lest we forget what? What is done for prevention? And if we forget, what are the consequences?

Look around. There is more conflict globally than there has ever been. Furthermore the majority of conflicts are not in the public eye, as the media gets to decide what is newsworthy. Even so, some questions are never asked, some are never answered.

Where are Gaddafi, Peres, and Nasser?

Why was Nixon on Howard Hughes's payroll? And so it goes.

Where did the money pledged for Haiti after the 2010 earthquake go?

I say to the people: Why allow yourself to be led? Be the change you seek.

The slaves were emancipated, but all they received was freedom. Freedom to starve and nowhere to live. At the same time, European settlers were given land to help them settle. The slaves had worked for free for 200 years and were given nothing.

Is this racism? Is it lack humanity? Is it greed?

Whatever it is - and it exists today in all different guises - it must stop. It's unacceptable. When the majority of individuals have their shoulders to the wheel of justice, then we will see significant movement forward.

There comes a time when it's necessary to become serious.

The negatives of the human condition - power, greed, fear, etc. - have prevailed and will exist. But they will be placed on an off-ramp to obscurity.

I urge everyone to reimagine themselves. As Naomi Klein said, the benefit of being part of a broader movement is knowing that some people are doing some things, and other people are doing other things, and nobody has to do everything.

Robert: Thank you, Herstel. You've certainly given us food for thought.

12

Visitors to mightyblue.com were encouraged to apply to the various groups which were listed, with brief descriptions regarding their activities.

Farmers of Abundance

Those dedicated to locating the supply chains and stocks globally, particularly the chains of waste. Their sources are acted on by the Networkers, who engineer the proper use and distribution of resources.

The Balancers

These are observers who operate in the background. They announce their presence with a double clap of the hands when some activity or action appears negative or amiss. They do not communicate otherwise. They slip away. When alerted those whose actions and goals are in need of review, are urged to visit Mighty Blue for guidance.

The Shadow

Members are anonymous and do not, as a rule, communicate directly with each other. They function through Herstel and identify themselves by a wipe of the face—double hands only when necessary - to alert others of their presence and, by implication of their potential influence in a given situation when assistance is needed. Members of the Shadow are everywhere but are mostly engaged in important positions in the existing ecosystem. They are the initial group of the transformation process, recruited by Herstel over a decade to realize the vision by offering access to the financial, political, legal, and economic bastions of global existence. Many are older and wiser, having realized that the absolute pursuit of wealth, power, and profit is an empty journey and wishing now to create a better future for the planet. They have replaced ego with service and give generously of their time and resources, which, collectively, are substantial.

The Networkers

These are regular ordinary people who have been given the opportunity and means to make their work more beneficial to the world at large. Using common sense, they increase efficiency, decrease waste, pursue service not profit, dissipate ego and judgement, and use their position to retool the governmental agencies and corporations for a more positive outcome. Networkers who face financial and management challenges when pursuing their goals find assistance to support themselves through Mighty Blue.

The Hackers

A group of technical wizards who offer the Networkers and Farmers of Abundance access to digital systems globally and without restriction. Tools provided by Herstel make it seamless for Hackers to access every network and insure it's impossible for their activity to be tracked. Although the targets may be aware of being compromised, they are powerless to do anything.

The Johnnies

This includes the entirety of people on the planet Mighty Blue. Every child and adult can pursue the replanting of the planet, from one tree to thousands. The positive effect on the environment will be self-evident.

The Resistors

There are those quite naturally who will push back against change. The majority of them exist on a plain of comfort – benefitting from the accident of their birth's geographical location - so resistance will be a kneejerk reaction. Fear eats the soul.

13

Monogram Coffee, Calgary, Alberta; May 2024

Alpha: Well, hello, my little IT wizard. Did you watch Herstel on No Hiding Place? Boy, I don't know about shaking up the world. More like smashing it to pieces. Imagine getting rid of organized religion. There will be a lot of unhinged people running scared and looking for shelter. And giving money to those in poverty. These are people who have never had money. They won't know what to do with it. Mind you, they won't have to worry. The gangs will relieve them of that. By the way, I'm thinking of getting a new car. I think I need a boost. Life has been monotonous lately.

Beta: Wish I had inherited wealth burning a hole in my pocket.

Alpha: Speaking of wealth, what are your thoughts on inherited wealth? Of course, a lot of the major estates - especially in Europe and United States - leads back to benefits from the slave trade, and with that we are into the reparations pot of soup where the temperature will continue to rise, when given the attention it needs. I mean a lot of the royal family's wealth would be part of that equation. How much are they worth? If most of that was given over, it would be a game changer for the Caribbean nations.

Beta: That's complicated! Old money - let's say fifteenth century to present age, passed on from generation to generation was extracted from the sweat of slaves and the resources of colonized countries. Then there's global corporate and technological investors, mostly a creation of smoke and mirrors and loss-making corporations who are the beneficiaries of the American capitalist system, a terribly sophisticated web of corruption, deceit, and greed that prints money when needed, underpinned by the American dollar, a de facto global currency with infinite legs. God forbid the dollar loses its global status, because the reality of living on debt will land on Americans, who will be forced to repay their debt or service the interest owed, at market rates. Middle class America will sink, and corporate America will partially drown. The perennial losers are the people and countries outside the power group who do not benefit from this fictitious wealth, except that they get to borrow from the pot and therefore contribute to it's growth and by extension the profits of the investors.

And we can't forget the IMF and World Bank, whose contributors and beneficiaries are the developed counties.

It's a self-defeating cycle that strengthens inequality and needs to be broken.

The first group – inheritors of old money - has benefited enough from the spoils. "Why should I have to answer for the previous generations wrongs?" they demand. "I wasn't around," they insist. Well, then you don't get to benefit from it either. Pay the reparations!

The latter group- the global financial institutions, including global corporations - are beneficiaries of a gross exploitation, which shouldn't be allowed.

No one should have unimaginable wealth. It's enough to have resources to meet your needs. Even a little more, God knows under what criteria. But the excess should be given to those in need.

Alpha: That's so fundamentally wrong. I don't want to work and struggle to pass the benefits to those who are only players, not contributors.

Beta: Come on! Most people work hard and struggle. How many do you know who simply leach off others? What're you working for, anyway? What's your goal? Money? Material possessions? What about the work? What value is it to you? What about prioritizing service, not profits? Why make profits the primary goal? If you're not taking it with you, what's the point? In your lifetime, how many cars can you drive? How many clothes can you wear? How much food can you eat?

Alpha: So we're back to tangling with the intangible? It's human nature to do the irrational and inexplicable. We're not creatures of low intelligence. We have intellect. Intelligence. We have free will to act as we please. Remember that. That's why we're so advanced. And not swinging from trees looking for a random banana. We learned how to create our own supplies. With accessibility!

Beta: We also have faith, right? Lots of it. Faith has been prominent for a long time. How's that working out, do you think, for such an intelligent lot?

Alpha: Your problem is you try to simplify everything. Life, humanity, the universe. It's all very complicated. You play with the cards you're dealt. Otherwise, you're just cheating. Nobody likes cheaters.

Beta: As I've said before, it's all about money. Money is power. There's no power without money. What do you think would be the impact of the global financial system if buying power were given to the least developed countries, if those countries were allowed the same proportionate debt as the developed countries? Here's some simple math to do tonight. When you've done the numbers, I'll be more interested in what your thoughts are.

How much corporate and private wealth is there in the world? Most of this wealth is dormant, you would agree. Not being actually used. Note the military spend $26 trillion each year on ways to kill us.

How much aid—civilian and government—is given each year? How is it distributed?

What's the net worth of the G20 countries?

What's the net-worth gap between the G20 and the rest? Then calculate the same for the G7 nations.

What would be the effect on everyone if that gap was closed?

Alpha: That's quite an interesting exercise. I'll try to have the answers for you next time. But you know what you're suggesting is impossible. It will devastate the value of everything. You can't have a functional world where there isn't much worth.

Beta: I think you're confusing value with wealth. How's your life measured? Does it have value? How's that measured? Does it have wealth? We know how that it's measured.

How would it effect you if those in poverty all over the world, including the developed world, were financially able and capable to grow their lives? Think about it.

14

Production meeting, BBC No Hiding Place Studio: May 2024

Following the interview, which had enjoyed viral distribution both via mainstream and social media, "Herstel" quickly became the most Googled word, and Robert had become introspective and subdued. He followed closely the development of the Herstel story, or at least that which was transparent. He also looked for signs of societal impact and change, as Herstel had stated that there was a lot going on behind the scenes, all of it orchestrated by individuals during their daily existence. Indeed, Robert had spent considerable time reimagining himself and played out in his mind what effect this would have on his work and personal life. It would be a game changer, as they said in the sports world. He was a man on the edge, contemplating the leap. As he listened to his colleagues and bosses he thought, "Don't push me, I'm close to the edge!"

Being discussed was the Dalai Lama, the interviewee for the next program.

Robert: What do we have on His Holiness? He has been invisible during the last ten years. Is there anything of major interest, or is he now simply an item on the bucket list of Hollywood stars, aging rock stars, and corporate leaders? Is he politically active in any way? How is his health?

Adam, raising his hand: Just one point to mention, which may not be relevant to this program and isn't included in production research notes. I'm told by a source in India that His Holiness has met Herstel Fidia several times during the past six months.

Robert listened and thought deeply about what he'd just heard. After a noticeably long period of silence, during which everyone waited intently for his response, he became animated.

Robert: Thank you. You're right. It's not relevant to this program. Can someone look into the arrival time of the Dalai Lama? I'd like to have an hour with him in the green room prior to the interview.

And to himself he mused "What an opportunity! What would Herstel and the Dalai Lama have to talk about? Certainly, the Dalai Lama would be forthcoming and candid if interrogated. What an opportunity indeed." He was very excited.

15

BBC Studio No Hiding Place (Green room) – May 2024 Interviewee: Dalai Lama

The Dalai Lama was comfortable and rested, enjoying a cup of tea and a few custard creams, of which he was particularly fond. He was in good spirits as Robert enters the room. It was their first meeting.

His Holiness, who was sitting on a large cushion on the floor, looked up at Robert's six-foot, four-inch frame and laughingly exclaimed, "My you are a big one!"

Robert joined the Dalai Lama on the floor with considerable effort and discomfort, which appeared to amuse his guest.

Robert: Thank you for agreeing to appear on our program. Are you comfortable? Do you have everything you need?

DL: I'm comfortable.

He had a twinkle in his eye, hinting at Roberts position on the cushion, as Robert was clearly not a yoga practitioner.

Robert: I use this time before the live interview to brief you on what to expect and also ascertain if there are any concerns or red flags you would care to share with me.

DL: This is sensible. I thank you. Since I left Tibet, I have no flags, needless to say a red one. (He laughs loudly at his own joke.) Do proceed.

Robert: A subject I'm quite interested in, though he's not something we will be discussing on the program—well, not this program at least—is the mysterious Herstel Fidia, whom I understand you've spent some time with.

I interviewed him a few months ago, and to be quite honest, I learned nothing of him. He spoke broadly and specifically of changes coming to our lives but was not forthcoming on details. What did you make of him? What did you talk about, if you don't mind me asking?

DL: I don't think he's from here. Here as we know it. This earthly plain. This planet. This time. He hasn't said so, but I sense it. I believe if that's so, he knows a lot more than we can imagine. That's a good case for paying attention to what he says and possibly playing whatever part we can.

The universe is in charge, Robert, don't forget that. We are important, yet insignificant. We bow to nature and follow meekly but happily, if we can.

Don't you like custard creams? How is it possible to get so much happiness from a biscuit? That's life, isn't it? Some need a large ten course meal to feel the same. We're complex, we humans. What's your custard cream Robert?

Robert: I was just thinking about that. What is it? Whatever it is, I haven't experienced it lately.

DL: When I met Herstel Fidia the very first time, I knew nothing of him. You know, the meeting was not pre-arranged. He just showed up. Now, after several meetings, I know a little more, but it's irrelevant. He just is. I felt we were two souls separated a long time ago, and here we were in conversation, as if no time had passed.

What did we talk about? I guess everything you're curious about. It's too vast and complex to be dealt with through investigative journalism. Also, it's not necessary for everyone to know. It's of no benefit to them. You wouldn't know what questions to ask. He's here, and everyone should listen to him carefully and take control of their lives, of their very existence. The future looks bright, Robert.

Robert: Again, you just said a lot, but as with Herstel, I've learned nothing.

DL: That's because you're interested in nothing. Therefore, all you will learn is nothing. Wake up, Robert. It's staring you in the face. (DL laughs loudly.)

Robert is troublingly puzzled.

DL: Okay, you'd like the elevator pitch, as they say in the United States. We think we need answers to everything, but to no avail. You drive your car, but do you know how it works? I presume not, but it doesn't prevent you from getting from A to B.

Herstel started on this journey some twenty years ago. Changing the course of humanity doesn't happen overnight, you know, Robert. (DL laughs loudly again.) His main objective is to free individuals to live with purpose for the benefit of themselves and others. He aims to dispose of our servile sheep mentality, to release us from the fear of not providing and not succeeding in the practices of inequality and waste. To assist with this process, he carefully created a number of groups to assist with the process. Who they are and what they do is not wholly transparent, but in essence, they cover all the bases for change. For example, the Shadow is an anonymous collection of power brokers and wealthy people who are on board to promote, and to provide support and influence when needed. Then there are the Hackers, who create access to every available network, including—and this is important—those of the criminal elements and the dark side who will be disabled. There are the Networkers, who manage the activities of those networks to the benefit of everyone. And the Balancers - ah, this is a tricky one - an anonymous group who secretly monitor the activities of all those connected to Mighty Blue and raise a red flag when it appears an action or activity is going off course. I'll get back to Mighty Blue in a moment.

The Farmers of Abundance track and monitor all the resources available on this abundant planet, and the Johnnies arrange and execute the planting of trees everywhere to alleviate ertain elements of climate change in no small way. There is another group—the Bushido. I'm not sure what they do. Herstel said they should be called the Angels of Mercy, as their work will release millions from present and future suffering.

How is all this possible? Mighty Blue, a portal of resources and data, which uses AI and software that Herstel stresses is eons ahead of the most advanced on the planet, is the manager and ringmaster. Fuel and energy is provided by the participation of individuals—millions of them—who are treading a parallel acceptable path in their daily lives and contributing to shifting the course of humanity.

Now, Robert, you have a vague idea. Does that help? You should simply join the wave and become a shining star.

Robert: When you review the changes he's talked about, and it's difficult to imagine how they will be executed. They are so wide ranging and complex, with all kind of consequences that you cannot fail to be overwhelmed by the size and scope of it all.

DL: But it's all plausible, Robert. Look at what's in place as we speak: racism, inequality, politics not serving the people, aid not getting to the needy. I can go on. As they stand, these issues are implausible, but it's what we live with. Why would change for the better be impossible or difficult?

Robert: Because there are those—the wealthy and powerful, the beneficiaries of the current status quo—who will oppose most or all of that which Herstel proposes. And they would be a tremendous force to overcome.

DL: Ah, the Resistors. Of course, there will be those who seek otherwise. It's human nature. There are those quite naturally who will push back against change. The majority exist on a plain of comfort, so resistance will be a knee-jerk reaction. Fear eats the soul.

Kindness, compassion and common sense will be deployed to address them if necessary. Typically, they will be tribal, not seeking rational discourse. Over time the blue wave will sweep many up. There will, however, remain those who hold out. Such is human nature.

. Herstel doesn't advise opposing the Resistors but aiding them in achieving their goals. Knowing their goals will be their first and probably unsurmountable obstacle. They will - not all - be a significant and constant number of crossovers. As I see it, a lot of the players who are part of the Shadow and their colleagues are warriors. We have a Trojan horse. We know how that turned out

Robert: Well, thank you for sharing that. Though, as you say, knowing how the engine works doesn't seem terribly relevant. I should concentrate on the driving, to extend the metaphor.

DL: You are a fan of cricket, Robert? You must be familiar with the work of the Trinidadian philosopher, CLR James. In particular, Beyond a Boundary. In it, he uses the phrase, "What do they know of cricket who only cricket knows?" Ponder that. (He laughs.) Spread your wings, Robert.

Robert: Thank you again for sharing. It has been enlightening. Thank you, your Holiness. Our interview begins in ten minutes.

16

THE CAGED BIRD SINGS
WITH A FEARFUL TRILL

Monogram Coffee, Calgary, Alberta: June 2024

Alpha: How are you today? You seem energized! Have you been paying much attention to the US election?

Beta: Not specifically. But it's hard not to notice. I do have a nagging concern that both the Republicans and the Canadian Conservatives, in their election, will triumph. Remember the support from the United States that the anti-vax truck drivers received. And the desire by Alberta Conservatives to isolate, Canada could become an innocent victim of the U.S. implosion.

Alpha: Ha-ha. I think you're being alarmist. After all, Alberta has a valid argument, and with a conservative government in Ottawa, the status quo will remain. It's Canada, for Christ's sake. We don't do civil unrest or revolution well. Now our neighbors to the south, that's a different matter. Americans love their reruns. So much so that we may very well see a replay of the Civil War. The average white man is beginning to feel fear. It's not rational, as white men they hold the reins of power and are by far the majority in the developed world. But they sense the inevitable, when they will be sidelined and when repayment for deeds previously done will be harsh and swift.

Beta: Now that's alarmist. Are you speaking as one of the herd?

Alpha: Ha-ha. As devil's advocate.

Beta: Well, this will either alarm you or send you into panic mode. This is about Herstel and the Mighty Blue. I've been doing hours of digging. There's now a tsunami of activity on the Internet, particularly on social media, and lots of excitement surrounding the events he predicted will occur. Which is intriguing as some of the proposed activities, activities that might be viewed as illegal or anarchic the majority of players see as positive. So, if you recall, Herstel talked about the Doctrine of Recovery, which has eighteen specific items to be executed or implemented. He said that the first project, so to speak, was the eradication of poverty. This will begin on July 26th, the opening day of the Summer Olympics, the operation Herstel refers to as Here Comes the Sun.

Alpha: Well, how is it going to be accomplished?

Beta: Get this. Everyone who falls under the umbrella of poverty will be provided with a smart phone. They will then be provided with funds - digital currency to enable them to purchase food and materials to facilitate adequate shelter. They will manage the use of the funds, which will be provided on a regular basis, and have the opportunity to start a business venture with the help of the Mighty Blue Bank. So we're talking eventually over one billion phones, at maybe two dollars fifty per phone, and an income supplement of between two to four dollars per day. How's your math? I make that about 500 billion a year initially, which will decrease as the impoverished get on their feet. To put that in perspective the world spent two and a half trillion on military equipment last year. Imagine what impact these actions will have financially and socially on every level.

Apparently, the organization of this has been in process for months and involves millions of people - all registrants of Mighty Blue who are using their existing positions to participate: computer techs, aid workers, exporters, shippers, civil servants. It's crazy.

Alpha: Goofy for sure. Where's the money coming from? Remember you said, or someone did, that only a tiny percentage—single digits—of the funds collected or pledged to aid organizations actually get to those who need them. The majority goes to the salaries and expenses of the administrators who are for the most part based in developed countries.

Oh, and the criminal element will think it's Christmas. There will be a national extortion day everywhere funds are sent. The organized crime outfits will hijack the funds or simply take from the poor.

Beta: Herstel has anticipated the criminal element and potential harm. However, he says we all have free will, and those who choose to do harm to their neighbour and community will be eaten by their own. The Angels of Mercy, some group or other, will ensure the criminal element will be knee-capped, as I think they say in that world.

Alpha: Sounds like the mafia! So if this is a solution, help us all.

17

Developing global news

Various other world leaders were, by the next morning, rendered irrelevant. The notes in backpacks were consistent. For the leaders of the Taliban: "Women have a rightful place. Don't stand in their way." In Iran: "Free yourself and your people." In Israel: "You are responsible for your own happiness, but not at the expense of the happiness of others." And in Saudi Arabia: "Who gets to decide on the relevance of a life?"

There was panic in some quarters. But the majority, felt the removal of a centuries-old shackle. It was a time for careful consideration. There was no rush to fill the void.

18

Olympic Opening Ceremony, Trocadero, Paris: July 26, 2024

It had been 100 years since Paris last hosted the Olympic games.

Excellence, respect, and friendship to build a better world were the main principles the founder of the modern games, Baron de Coubertin, cherished.

France had chosen to move the opening ceremony out of the traditional stadium setting and onto the banks of the Seine, 160 boats carrying over 10,000 athletes and delegates from 206 countries, were cheered by over 600,000 spectators, most of whom were attending the ceremony for free. A billion viewers on television witnessed this resounding success.

At the end of the six- kilometre route, over 120 heads of state, sovereigns and heads of government gathered at the Trocadero for the usual speeches and the official start of the games.

The President of the Organizing Committee, a picture of triumph, got things rolling, followed by the IOC president, looking relieved as he usually does. "We can begin on time and we have avoided any disasters."

When he finished his speech, instead of introducing the heads of state to officially declare the games open, he introduced the Ambassador of the

Mighty Blue. The media were stunned, but the President and others at the podium offered Herstel a warm welcome.

"Today is a beautiful day for humanity. Are you all enjoying this glorious ceremony?"

He paused as a rising wave of cheering reached a crescendo.

"I want to leave you with a few thoughts. Just a few. How many of you remember the Kenyan athlete Kip Keino? He and his brothers lit up the Mexican Olympics in 1968 with their exuberance and talent. Before that time, African, Caribbean, and some Asian countries did not participate in the Olympics in any significant manner, as any local athlete deemed good enough would represent the country of his rulers. Independence came to most of those counties in the 60s, and they created their own representation. And look where we are now! You see now that the Haitians and Palestinians and others at similar disadvantage are not lesser athletes. They simply need the opportunity.

In 1937, Churchill said of the Palestinians, 'I do not agree that the dog in a manger has the final right to the manger even though he may have lain there for a very long time. I do not admit that. I do not admit that a great wrong has been done to the Red Indians of America or the black people of Australia. I do not admit that a wrong has been done to these people by the fact that a stronger race, a higher-grade race, a more worldly—wise race to put it that way—has come in to take their place.' He was wrong. Was he not?"

Deafening cheers fill the air.

"There were many wrongs done to many by Mr. Churchill and his ilk. For humanity this destructive arc, those wrongs have to corrected and prevented in future. We begin with one half of the population who have been subjugated for thousands of years without rhyme or reason. The Baha'i Faith addresses this succinctly, "The world of humanity is possessed of two wings: the male and the female. So long as these two wings are not equivalent in strength, the bird will not fly. Until womankind reaches the same degree as man, until she enjoys the same arena of activity, extraordinary attainment for humanity will not be realized; humanity cannot wing its way to heights of real attainment.

Many wonder why there's a need for so much aid. When reparations are in place, the need for aid will diminish. Someone once said, "if you give a man a fish, you feed him for a day. If you teach him to fish, he'll feed himself for a lifetime." Large sectors of the human population, for hundreds of years, were not taught to fish. In fact, they were kept away from the rivers and beaten with the fishing rod.

Today, I announce that reparations will begin for all of those communities across the world who are deserving. This isn't simply payments but also the re-structuring of laws and systems, which were knowingly or not, created to ensure the disadvantaged remained that way.

Today all aid—civil and government aid—will be re-chanelled to ensure it all goes to the intended recipients. Under the existing system, only 1% of all aid actual reach those in need.

All those who fall under the umbrella of poverty in the developed and less developed world will begin to receive funding to lift themselves out of the poverty trap. We begin to eradicate poverty.

Aid recipients will also be given financial tools to manage funds they receive.

We're going to lift everyone up. Those who give and those who receive.

Today, many people on our planet can sing 'Here Comes the Sun.'

In the spirit of the Olympic charter, we're building a better world for everyone.

Respect, excellence, and friendship."

Warm but subdued applause followed. Then intense discussions broke out everywhere.

The French President drew a curtain on the proceedings by declaring the Summer Olympics XXXIII open.

IOC President: Herstel, before you disappear, as you tend to do (he smiles questioningly), I have a favour to ask. My granddaughter—her name is Sylvie—is pursuing a social careers course at Paris X11 University. No, I don't know what that is. But she's very passionate about social rights and the environmental struggle, which she believes are complementary. I confess that prior to the ceremony, I shared with her that you would appear here today. She was beside herself and begged for a few moments with you to ask what she described as 'the millions of questions the world wants answers to.' I know it's a big ask. And I warn you, she hopes to share whatever she learns in an article for Le Monde, where she's a part time gofer.

Herstel: She sounds very smart and proactive. I will chat with her. The time is right.

IOC President: Wait here. I will find her and a private space for you both. Thank you, Herstel.

Herstel: I believe the gratitude is all mine.

IOC President: Maybe when I chat with Sylvie, I'll learn something about you. He winked and smiled. They shook hands.

Sylvie and Herstel met in the back of her granddad's SUV, as finding a quiet space in the midst of the proceedings proved impossible. Sylvie was anxious to make good use of her time and dove straight in.

Sylvie: Reparations. That's so complicated, emotional, and global, and you say it has begun. How? Where will we see it manifest itself? Where are the funds coming from? That's the most controversial aspect.

Herstel: Well, firstly it becomes less complicated and controversial if we all accept it's a reality and worked toward a solution. More importantly, we all need to be trusting and truthful.

The Church of England recently acknowledged that it may have had a hand in facilitating slavery. Its solution is to make available 100 million pounds for research into the matter. The people of the Caribbean, who were most impacted by that part of the slave trade would respond, 'Ah wasn't barn yesterday!' You see, there's no shortage of funds. The obstacle is the lack of desire to deal with the issue in an honest manner.

We know where the funds are, and we will access and distribute them as see necessary. AI is a major part of all we do. It allows the facts to dominate and removes emotion from decisions.

Yes, I know you want to know more about this. What sums are we talking about with regards to reparations and poverty? Billions of dollars, I believe. Now take any one of the top tech start-ups from the past few years. They raise billions and operate at a loss during their early years. No one in the public worries about where the money is coming from and what happens to it. So think of reparations as start-up funds. Same for aid. Only that's easier to understand, as the funds are there. It's just that they are being largely misused.

Your granddad mentioned you might be submitting an article to Le Monde about our discussion, so let me give you some context.

Let's firstly deal with reparations. America freed the slaves in 1863 and gave them nothing to get started on—no money, no land. At the same time they were giving millions of acres away to the white peasants from Europe. They were willing to give the Europeans an economic base but were unwilling to do the same for the Africans who were brought against their will in chains to the United States and worked free for nearly 250 years. So emancipation for the slave was freedom to be hungry, without shelter and without land to cultivate. In tandem with Churchill's view, here is the official American policy toward acquisition of Indian lands:

The United States, while intending never to acquire lands from the Indians other than peaceably and with their free consent, may require to reclaim from the state of nature, providing for the support of millions of civilized beings, will not violate any dictate of justice or of humanity, for they will give to the few thousand Indigenous scattered over that territory an ample equivalent for any right they may surrender, but will always leave them the possession of lands more than they can cultivate, and more than adequate to their subsistence, comfort, and enjoyment.

There's a substantial history of the United States government providing financial assets to white citizens, but not to Black citizens. Let's go back to the period in which there was a promise made of forty-acre land grants to Black Americans. At the same time, when that the US government failed to fulfill that promise, it gave one and a half million white families in the United States one hundred and sixty-acre land grants in the western territories, under the Homestead Act of 1860. That was a transfer that has resulted in the situation in which forty-five million living white Americans are continuing to be beneficiaries of those land patents.

The British paid slave owners when slavery was abolished.

The Slave Compensation Act 1837 was why that money was borrowed and paid for by the taxpayer to compensate slave owners in the British colonies of the Caribbean, Mauritius, and the Cape of Good Hope in the amount of approximately £20 million for freed, enslaved Africans. Ex-enslaved Africans received NO monetary compensation. For example, George Hibbert of the West India Company received £63,000, which is the equivalent to more than £49 million in today's money.

What is interesting is Germany has paid compensation for the Holocaust up to 2018. Over $86 billion Japan paid the U.S. until the seventies for the Pearl Harbour attack.

The Haitian government paid France and the United States 40% of their national income for 122 years to compensate for freeing themselves. They were considered a loss of assets to those countries.

There has never been financial compensation to slaves for their losses for 500 years of enslavement and colonialism.

In 1825, France, backed by several warships, demanded from Haiti 150 million francs as indemnity for claims over the loss of property during the revolution and, in addition, for diplomatic recognition as an independent state. Reparations for the loss of their property - their slaves.

The debt choked Haiti's economic development as interest mounted, snatching a significant share of GDP and restricting development. Haiti was forced to take loans from Crédit Industrial et Commercial bank, enriching French shareholders. The remainder of Haiti's debt was financed by the National City Bank of New York, now Citibank, and in 1915, U.S. President Woodrow Wilson responded to complaints from U.S. banks about Haiti's debts by invading that country. Never had a country been invaded for owing debts. The American occupation lasted until 1934 and was deeply resented by Haitians who staged numerous revolts. France finally repealed the debt in 2016, but no reparations were forthcoming despite being the root cause of Haiti's decimation.

Now Haiti is an aid state, almost totally dependent on foreign governments and institutions and remittances from the diaspora. Its underdevelopment can be attributed to corruption and geopolitical manipulation. And let's not forget the opportunistic siphoning of aid by the very agencies that collect donations from around the world. (Kenneth Mohammed, Intelligence Sanctuary)

The American abolitionist and statesman Frederick Douglas in 1852 succinctly summarized the residual effects of the Doctrine of Discovery for the colonial masters: "The rich inheritance of justice, liberty, and prosperity and independence bequeathed by your fathers is shared by you not by me."

One hundred and seventy years later, the wealth gap is worse now than it was then.

In 2013 the economic consulting firm Brattle Group, engaged to build an economic framework to facilitate reparations, produced a 115-page report in 2023 dissecting the complex aftermath of slavery. They calculated the true cost—not only the economics but also the intangibles: the harrowing loss of liberty and life; the stolen potential of forgone earnings; and the deprivation that reverberates across centuries. Intergenerational trauma, loss of heritage, and disparities in life expectancy, employment opportunities, and income is all meticulously analyzed.

Particularly incisive is its calculation of cumulative wealth and GDP amassed by nations that exploited African labour. This approach delves into the systemic enrichment of European countries, showing a web of culpability beyond individual actions. Another striking feature is the report's dissection of the enslavement and post-enslavement eras. The estimated figure of total repatriation costs £103 trillion exceeds the 2019 annual collective GDP of the world.

Brattle's research highlights the £20 million paid to British enslavers in 1833, an amount that translates to £17 billion today. This compensation, extracted through a Bank of England loan, continued to be shouldered up to 2015 by British taxpayers, including the Windrush generation and other descendants of enslaved people. It is a stark reminder of the unbroken chains that bind the present to a past that must be reconciled.

And what about aid? Smoke and mirrors ?

The United Nations chief Guterres recently observed that 'our global financial system was designed by wealthy countries, largely to their benefit. Deprived of liquidity, many of the least developed countries are locked out of capital markets by predatory interest rates."

With poorer states trapped in a "perfect storm for perpetuating poverty and injustice," Guterres said the least developed countries require a "minimum" of $500 billion a year to help them overcome their problems, build up job-creating industries, and repay debts.

The fundamental problem with philanthropy is a lack of understanding and feeling for those who are designated recipients. There's no equality. "I am giving this to you. You need to do this to make yourself better." The giver doesn't have skin in the game.

We're constantly fed the images of starving children in Africa. Always Africa. The richest continent on the planet is always referred to as one country. Henry Kissinger proposed in the 1970s that the U.S. plan to restrict the population growth of Africa to ensure that more of its resources were available for use in the west.

The Alliance for Food Sovereignty shares their view on the food shortage problem:

"The world currently produces enough food to adequately feed all the Earth's inhabitants, yet those in the West fundamentally misdiagnose the problem as relating to low productivity; we do not need to increase production as much as ensure more equitable access to food."

And there's a further problem. About one-third of the world's food is lost or wasted every year. And the United Nation's Food and Agriculture Organization estimates that everything that's lost or wasted is enough to feed one and a quarter billion hungry people each year.

But businesses have a part to play too. More than a quarter of all food waste comes from restaurants, while 13% comes from retailers.

Seemingly benevolent foundations continue to fund and push restrictive seed legislation that limits and restricts crop innovation to well-resourced labs and companies. These initiatives don't increase widespread innovation but rather contribute to the privatization and consolidation of corporate monopolies over seed development and seed markets.

The problem is further complicated because the costs of land and labour as well as infrastructure are socially and politically produced. Africa is, in fact, highly productive—it's just that the profits are realized elsewhere. Through colonization, neoliberalism, debt traps and other forms of legalized pillaging, African lives, environments, and bodies have been devalued and made into commodities for the benefit and profit of others. Infrastructure has been designed to channel these commodities outside of the continent itself. Africa isn't self-sufficient in cereals because its agricultural, mining, and other resource-intensive sectors have been structured in ways that are geared toward serving colonial and then international markets, rather than African peoples themselves.

There is no shortage of practical solutions and innovations by African farmers and organizations. We invite those corporations in the West who are guided by profit to step back and learn from those on the ground. The current system is broken.

- Today, only 1% of all the money intended to end poverty (official development aid and humanitarian assistance combined), goes directly to the extreme poor.
- Only 1% of all official development assistance (funding from agencies such as US Aid and UK Aid) and an even smaller portion (0.4% in 2018) of all international humanitarian assistance (all charitable funding included), goes directly to grassroots organizations in the Global South.
- In 2018, only 5.2% of the $9 billion (£7.5 billion) in U.S. foundation funding earmarked for sub-Saharan Africa went to local organizations
- That means about 99% of anti-poverty funding stays in the hands of the global development sector, which means Western agencies.

There are millions of well-meaning people who genuinely want to make the world a better place and help people escape poverty but who have been conditioned into believing that the only way to do it is by safely placing that support far from the poor themselves, being careful not to work with them directly on the premise that the African poor are wannabe fraudsters.

Mighty Blue will enable well-meaning people to refocus, re-organise and be more productive with their efforts.

Only those perceived as the most legit people—those from the Global North—are allowed at the helm. For example, after the 2010 Haiti earthquake, this is what was being said in Forbes: "Don't send money overseas. Even though Haiti is a foreign disaster, don't send a donation to a foreign bank account. Experts say this is never legit."

There is no such thing as humans who are more legitimate than others. We are all the same. The only thing that makes us different is opportunity, or the lack of it. (African Visionary Fund)

The term foreign aid is a misnomer. It's usually not aid, and it's not given to foreign countries. With aid agencies, a lot of the funds go to staff, salaries, and travel, and aid material is purchased in the donor country. People believe that so much money should fix everything, but a lot of the money that is pledged is never delivered.

Sylvie, I hope that is enough for you to get started. You must try to integrate what you write with your own thoughts and observations. It was a pleasure meeting you. I wish you well for the future."

19

Associated Press, Tokyo, Japan; July 30, 2024,

In a bizarre incident yesterday, the leader of North Korea was killed when a short range ballistic missile (SRBM) reversed its course after launch and returned to the launch site. There were a number of unconfirmed causalities. No official statement has at yet been issued by the state.

20

THE BLUE WAVE

Monogram Coffee, Calgary, Alberta; July 2024

Alpha: Did you order ahead? Smart!

Beta: That's why they pay me the big bucks.

The friends settle down comfortably after Alpha is served his drink. He would never order online, as the ordering of his drink in person is a major part of hiss coffee experience. He's keen to impress the barista with his vast knowledge of coffee, which manifests in his considering, aloud, every possible combination of drink and describing their taste before settling on the same drink he orders every time.

Alpha: What have you been up to? You've been missing for almost two months.

Beta: I've been surfing the Blue Wave. It's difficult to comprehend. Everyone connected to Mighty Blue seems to be on a high. We have all taken a deep breath and feel literally free, though there's still so much to do. But the results are so positive, the positive energy is overwhelming.

Alpha: Did you say "we?" Are you part of this cult? Listen to me. This is dangerous. All of the norms as we know them are being threatened. So what do you think is going on?

Beta is circumspect: I think the fundamental goodness of humanity is finally ascending over the fearful and selfish elements that have until now been allowed to dominate. With Mighty Blue, each individual is able to positively and collectively contribute to the good, and they outnumber those who have been mis-led. Finally, joy is the leading star, not power or money or greed. Material goods and instant gratification are relegated to their proper place. Necessary but not to be worshiped.

21

Production Meeting for the Oxfam UK President Interview, No Hiding Place Studio: August 30, 2024

The evening prior, Robert stepped away from his laptop and stood up. He could see clearly now, having mulled over the contents of his discussion with the Dalai Lama. He had just spent a good two hours on Mighty Blue reimaging himself, as millions were doing globally.

Now he knew what was important. Also, he knew which meaningless goals and activities should be cast aside. He felt alive and energized. He saw opportunities and possibilities everywhere he looked. Clouds of negativity and subconscious fear had parted and were dissipating. Today, when he stepped into the meeting, the production team was surprised by his energy, his evident joie de vivre.

Robert: Okay! How are you all?

Caught off guard, they offered no answer. Adam laughed and looked around at everyone. He sensed a shift, and was excited to see what would transpire.

Robert: We're going to chart a new course with our interviews. We're going to bare the truth and throw out the political and the bullshit. We will not tread softly; we will stomp around. There will be hurt egos, damaged reputations, and angry people. So be it. It's a complete makeover. So prepare your research accordingly. I'm not interested in the obvious, the trite, the self-publicity, or the polishing of egos. I want to know what people are doing to assist with the positive surge of humanity. Or more importantly—and this is where you come in—what are they doing to prevent positive steps?

The president of Oxfam. What better place to start? I hazard a guess most of what I have here is irrelevant and self-aggrandizing. So burn the midnight oil and let me have something substantial for tomorrow. Let's have some fun. Let's make our lives meaningful. Any questions?

They all hurried off to get started, feeling the wind lift their steps.

22

Interview with Oxfam UK President, No Hiding Place Studio; September 7, 2024

Robert: Welcome to NHP. You're currently the leader of one of the major charities in the world. Your background makes you a perfect fit for the job, and I'll get to that in a moment. My main question is this: how will your agency differ in its practice today from what transpired during the past two decades? What were the achievements then, what do you plan on achieving going forward and how will you do that? Now, while you ponder that, I just want to give the viewers a quick glance at your CV, so to speak.

On paper, if anyone can create a positive path forward for aid agencies, you would seem well equipped. However, in your previous positions, all in the aid world, it was very much more of the same. You took over the steering wheel and simply kept the vehicle moving forward on its same course. There was no evidence of change. Indeed, the results of those organizations over the past decade before your tenure would suggest they were failing operations. Yet you chose to maintain the status quo. What does that say of the expectation of your current position? I imagine most of those you were dedicated to helping would be hard pressed to know what these organizations were, what they did, and how successful they were. Now, with a leading UK charity, you have global exposure, and it leads me to question what these organizations are achieving, save providing good jobs for the administrators.

Oxfam President: The reality is, the global need is so great that it is a struggle to stay on top of it even with the kind of funds the public is so generously donating.

Robert: Yes, I know. Your donations were over 400 million dollars last year. Is this really about the numbers? If the total budget of all of the charities was applied at once to eliminate poverty and hunger, would it be successful? If not, why? Now here are some rough figures. The United Nations believes it would take 55 billion dollars a year to eradicate poverty and hunger. The total aid budget - civil and government - is 850 billion dollars What say you? Is the challenge delivery? Maybe Herstel Fidia has the answers.

I understand that he intends to provide directly to those in need, the funds they require to buy food and materials to alleviate hunger, and to provide adequate means of shelter. How this will be done, we don't know. But on the face of it, does that sound feasible? And does that render aid organizations and charities redundant?

Oxfam President: I've been following the revelations of Herstel. I believe that in his solutions, the existing aid administration network will play a significant part. As you say, we don't know.

Robert: Well, the future certainly looks interesting. With or without the Herstel factor. Do you know if anyone in the aid sector has been in conversation with Herstel? I believe the implementation of his operation is already on the way. And for you as the new head of this organization, do you plan a major change of operation or to simply ensure that what exists is more efficient financially and in its delivery.

Oxfam President: That is my plan initially.

Robert: Well, we will wait and see.

The interview continues with the President sharing his views on the political nature of aid and the difficulty of engineering positive change to a system modelled for decades on a do-good feel-good beggar's handout scenario. Somewhat thrown off guard by Roberts approach, he found solace in sharing his journey as a refugee who sailed through the top educational establishment in Australia, with honours, and into coveted positions in the aid world. Oddly, he appeared to be a man in therapy realizing he was a victim of the system, disarmed by his personal achievements. He left the interview wondering what his life's goals were. Did he have any? Were they forgotten in the glittering lights?

Robert: Thank you, Sir.

They shook hands.

They both felt uncomfortable.

23

Herstel Fidia's Address to the United Nations Assembly, New York: September 13, 2024

The sound of Tingsha Tibetan bells filled the room as an elegant figure in a blue gown approached the podium. No introduction - as he requested - but everyone knew who he was, and the audience was larger than normal. There was a sense of expectation. All major news networks were for the first time broadcasting the live feed from UN Web TV. The world was watching.

On arrival, Herstel scanned the delegates slowly and deliberately from left to right before his attention returned to the centre of the room. He paused for a minute, then he began:

This organization—and I'm not going to say anything no one's aware of— is unique in its responsibility for the peace and safety of this planet and its inhabitants.

Sadly, those who created it also ensured in its rules of operation that they were more equal than the rest. Essentially, the United Nations exists to prevent the bullying of nations by other nations. The one missing ingredient is consequence: there are no deterrence. The wolves have taken residence in the henhouse.

There are numerous plans and targets. Okay. Implementation, well, not so much.

The security council is the manifestation of insanity. It's responsible for ensuring international peace and security, but in operation, prevents peace and is an observer of conflicts. It's a mountain expedition bus with a steering wheel but no brakes. The passengers have to implement a braking system to ensure a safe and progressive journey.

Reforming the security council will happen when the interests of all groups are given equal opportunity.

The power must not lie with the developed and powerful. Power tends to corrupt. Absolute power corrupts absolutely, as Lord Acton said. Stop living in the past. The 1945 membership rules are beyond obsolete.

Herstel relaxed, performed some ska dance steps, and began singing.

"Better think of your future,
Time to straighten right out,
A message to you—and you."

He then started rapping:

"I am not here to
articulate nor pontificate.
The treason was the reason,
treason to the state of the human race.
A group of Judases seized the day
and the centuries.
They grabbed and stabbed.
They hoarded and branded
the stamp on the heads of the brothers to be elevated.
They knew it was wrong.
They knew it would make them strong/stronger/strongest.
Not just them. But their heirs, even though they didn't care.
Why am I here?
I am the essence.
I am the sense.

Now we can remove the hand that tips the scale.
Now we can embrace what's real.
Who am I?
Who are the IMF, World Bank, and World Economic Forum?

He stopped rapping and with a grin, continued:

It's all about economic power and these organizations—elected or not—control vast amounts of the economic power of the planet. I have no skin in the game. I'm merely shining light on a more enlightened path for humanity. Life is beautiful. Life is sacred, it's often said. But for whom?

Have a say. Have a hand in making your life worthwhile.

Everything I'm about to express to you is self-evident. Understand it will all become real. It's just a matter of time. Humanity needs to shake off the shackles of servility and diminish the desire to be led. Humanity must now turn to the power of the individual. For self- and others' service. It's your responsibility to investigate the truth. Don't believe all you are told.

Challenge the status quo—pit's not working.

This is the future of humanity. There will be no wavering from the course. The only variance is that of time—some will embrace this truth now, and some later. Where are we going? To a peaceful and happy existence. How will we get there? By using the guidelines that appear in the Doctrine of Recovery, details of which I'm about to reveal. The Doctrine of Recovery will rescue us from the pitfalls of the Doctrine of Discovery.

Let me be specific. From this point on, we must all endeavour to reimagine ourselves, our communities, our work, our plans, our lives.

Humanity, this is 2024. You shouldn't be where you are now. You know this. You have somehow jumped off the proper course. We're going to collectively get us back on track. I'll remind you what's not right. I'll explain how it's being fixed. We've done the prep work. Now the heavy lifting begins. This involves everyone on the planet.

Everyone! Everyone is a consumer. Everyone who works can have a say in some way.

We come not to judge. What is done is done. Now we must repair and move on.

There will, however, be a degree of reckoning. Those who deliberately orchestrate the unnecessary suffering of others through free will, free speech, or intellectual gymnastics will pay for their actions. The piper will be the neighbour, the friend, the community.

We are united by a determination to defend cooperation among our countries, free national and social development, sovereignty, security, equality, and self-determination. We're associated with one another in the endeavour to change the current system of international relations which is based on injustice, inequality, and oppression. We must act on international policy as a global independent factor.

It's necessary to eliminate the abysmal inequality that separates developed and developing countries. Otherwise, we'll continue to struggle to eliminate the poverty, hunger, disease, and illiteracy that hundreds of millions of human beings are still experiencing.

We require a new world order based on justice, equality, and peace to replace the unfair and unequal system that prevails today under which wealth continues to be concentrated in the hands of a few powers whose economies, based on waste, are maintained thanks to the exploitation of workers and to the transfer and plundering of natural and other resources of countries in Africa, Latin American, and other regions of the world.

When one analyzes the structure of the contemporary world, it's confirmed that numerous rights of all peoples still are not guaranteed.

The collective has always affirmed its abhorrence of racial discrimination and pogroms of any kind. Deep in our hearts, we repudiate with all our strength the unrelenting persecution and genocide that Nazism unleashed in its time against the Jewish people.

Do we not see a similarity in contemporary history with the eviction, persecution, and genocide carried out today against the Palestinian people, stripped of their land and expelled from their own homes?

Arms expenses are irrational. They should cease, and these funds should be used to finance development. The current international monetary system is bankrupt and should be replaced. The debts of countries that are relatively less developed and in disadvantageous situations are unbearable and cannot be resolved.

Mr. President, distinguished representatives, there's often talk of human rights, but it's also necessary to speak of the rights of humanity. Why should some people walk around barefoot so that others can travel in luxurious automobiles? Why should some live for thirty-five years so that others can live for seventy? Why should some be miserably poor so that others can be overly rich?

I speak in the name of the children in the world who do not have a piece of bread. I speak in the name of the sick who do not have medicine. I speak on behalf of those whose rights to life and human dignity have been denied. Some countries have access to the sea; others do not. Some have energy resources; others do not. Some have abundant lands on which to grow food; others do not. Some are so saturated with machines and factories that their citizens cannot even breathe the air of their poisoned atmosphere; others have nothing more than their emaciated arms with which to earn their bread.

At this point, an American delegate whispered to his Ambassador: "This is Castro's 1979 address to the United Nations. Verbatim."

U.S. ambassador: "Get the secretary of state on the line. We should get advice on whether we stay."

"In other words," Hertsel continued, "some countries have abundant resources; others have none. What is the destiny of the latter? To starve to death? To be eternally poor? Of what use, then, is civilization? What is the use of humanity's conscience? Of what use is the

United Nations? Of what use is the world?

It's not possible to speak of peace in the name of tens of millions of human beings throughout the world who die yearly of hunger, of curable disease. One cannot speak of peace in the name of 900 million illiterate persons. The exploitation of poor countries by rich countries must cease. I know that in many poor countries there are also exploiters and that the exploited can also be found in rich countries

I'm addressing the rich nations. I'm addressing the poor countries. Enough of words. Deeds are needed. Enough of abstractions. Specific actions are needed.

A set of global goals was developed by the United Nations, in consultation with world leaders, international organizations and the general public to help combat startling facts like those I have presented. These Sustainable Development Goals aim to confront the biggest issues affecting our world today. These goals are:

1. *End poverty in all its forms everywhere.*
2. *End hunger, achieve food security and improved nutrition, and promote sustainable agriculture.*
3. *Ensure healthy lives and promote well-being for all at all ages.*
4. *Ensure inclusive and quality education for all and promote lifelong learning.*
5. *Achieve gender equality and empower all women and girls and others who have been disempowered*
6. *Ensure access to clean water and sanitation for all.*
7. *Ensure access to affordable, reliable, sustainable, and modern energy for all.*
8. *Promote inclusive and sustainable economic growth, employment, and decent work for all.*
9. *Build resilient infrastructure, promote sustainable industrialization, and foster innovation.*
10. *Reduce inequality within and among countries.*
11. *Make cities inclusive, safe, resilient, and sustainable.*
12. *Ensure sustainable consumption and production patterns.*
13. *Take urgent action to combat climate change and its impacts.*
14. *Conserve and sustainably use the oceans, seas, and marine resources.*
15. *Sustainably manage forests, combat desertification, halt and reverse land degradation, and halt biodiversity loss.*
16. *Promote just, peaceful, and inclusive societies.*
17. *Revitalize the global partnership for sustainable development.*

The aim is for these goals to be achieved by 2030.

I assure you that, with the help of every individual focused on positive action and production and with the resources of Mighty Blue, these goals will be achieved sooner.

Now is the time to plant your footsteps firmly in the sand.

The sound of weapons, of threatening words and their prepotency in the international arena must cease. Enough of the illusion that the world's problems can be solved with nuclear weapons. Bombs might kill the hungry, the sick, and the ignorant, but they cannot kill hunger, disease, ignorance, and the people's just rebellion. In the holocaust, the wealthy will also die.

They are the ones that stand to lose the most in this world. Let us say farewell to arms and concentrate in a civilized manner on the most urgent problems of our time. This is the responsibility and most sacred duty of every statesman in the world. Furthermore, this is the indispensable requirement for humanity's survival.

Following the last war, you talk about 75 years of peace. Is this really so? A member of the Security Council invades another country and kills thousands of innocent people, yet they stride the world stage unobstructed. This is simply wrong. Wrong does not come in different shades. This must not happen again. This will not happen again.

The current ecosystem, born partially of the Document of Discovery, has to be changed.

We have the resources, ingenuity, and resilience to move humanity onto a positive arc.

Generally, the people - those who seek truth, want a better playing field. But political will and economic disparity stand in the way. We can do better. We will do better. A blue wave is coming. We have begun. We are doing this. You can do this. You are doing this. Now we must pick up the pace.

The United Nations must pursue truth and justice. There is no room for those who seek other paths. They will withdraw and embrace each other allowing the rest to move forward in peace and happiness. The shackles of colonialism embedded in organized religion must be broken. In Africa and Latin America, lives are too controlled by religion which benefits from the exploitation of fear and power to the reward a few. The developed countries have shifted away from this system. Greater economic success, though not the premier goal in the ideal world, is the result.

As Herstel spoke, sounds of disruption echoed throughout the chamber. The Russian delegation was in disarray, and they all left. They had just learned that their head of state had been shot. Herstel continued:

How will these changes be sustained? By following the Doctrine of Recovery, which in essence adjusts the Doctrine of Discovery. Presented by the Pope in the fifteenth century, the Doctrine of Discovery became the basis for a global financial, social and economic system which continues to function today. The pope will rescind that document which will work in the interest of humanity and especially so for Indigenous and First Nations people.

The Doctrine of Recovery contains some essential requirements attuned by common sense and truth, self-evident and necessary for the progress of humanity in a peaceful and co - operative manner.

Although not yet apparent in some cases, all aspects of the Doctrine of Recovery are interrelated. Furthermore, they are all in progress. I shall summarise them for you:

Eradicate poverty and hunger.

Remove the mask of racism.

Reduce civilian gun ownership.

Reverse climate change.

Hold politicians legally accountable.

Begin payment of reparations and reform prejudicial laws and systems.

Eradicate modern slavery.

Limit inherited wealth.

Share corporate profits with all workers.

Create more efficient delivery system for humanitarian aid, and do not use it for military purchases.

Abolish organized religion.

Ensure freedom of movement for refugees.

Create a global peacekeeping force.

Reduce national military stockpiles.
Create a global response unit for natural disasters.
Phase out borders and nationalism.
Provide comprehensive care for mental health patients.
Disable the illegal production and distribution of drugs.
Pay realistic incomes to people in the entertainment and sports industries.
Plan for a global shift to a plant-based diet.

And there you have it. I expect a myriad of questions and criticisms. Understand these changes are necessary and in progress.

One important question regards the criminal element hijacking funds intended for poverty relief, reparations, and aid. Once identified, simply by their actions, Mighty Blue will facilitate the draining of the financial resources of criminals and scrub their digital IDs.

Servility brought us here. Servility will put us back on track as we look to serve ourselves to the benefit of all. We are redistributing the wealth and resources of the planet to the good of all. Some of you may feel—as is human nature—that you wish to devote your energies to counter the positives. Feel free. Our recourses are infinite and impregnable.

Tomorrow is September 14, 2024. Mark this date. There will be a global demonstration against the pursuit of military solutions in the face of human problems We all know this.

September 14 - Something to look forward to and keep you engaged.

On the universal question of firearms and the military, there exists supply enough to eradicate the human race many times over. As a civilian, what can you achieve with firearms?

Kill someone? Kill yourself? Fight your government?

To governments, very shortly all military capability will be disabled for 24 hours to give you pause for thought. Organized protection on a global scale to the benefit of the majority is the proper path.

On the challenging topic of racism, legislation is a band aid. It is an adult disease which we must stop infecting our children with. This is an individual ailment and must be treated accordingly. There are times when people need to look in the mirror and face themselves without fear. It takes strength to accept the truth of our own failings.

As Sting said, I love her, but she loves someone else.

Herstel paused for a moment before beginning a slow rap:

"Glutton for nuttin'.
Honey not money.
Body to earth.
Rust to dust.
Blindness to excess.
Happiness into the abyss.
Kindness bypassed.
Compassion my ass.
Empty as a bottomless pit.
That's it.
Pour some more.
I need some more, darling.
I consume for feeling.
Deaf and blind when we ask it.
Will you listen from your casket?"

He bowed and bid his farewell, *"Your future is in your hands. Mighty Blue is behind you. Conduct yourself with honour."* Then he exited the chambers.

The spokesperson for the president of the General Assembly, who was expected to deliver a briefing after the speech stood at the podium and stared at the floor. There was a lull in proceedings. And universal silence.

24

"All systems down!"

The cry rang out across the planet as military systems in every country without exception were discovered to be inoperative. Emergency back-up systems offered no rescue.

Initially, the major powers looked to each other, assuming some threat of attack. Armed forces with hand weapons were mobilised and put on alert. There was very little offensive power – ground or arial – available.

The military might of the planet was dialled back a hundred years.

It was a day to pause and think. How was this possible? Every investigation drew a blank. Paranoia raised its ugly head. What if we are disabled and others aren't?

During his speech at the UN, Herstel had promised this demonstration as a reminder that military conflict is futile.

The logical step forward would be collective disarmament.

This Herstel explained was a painful choice for those imbedded in defence and the arms industry but, he stressed. Collective disarmament is inevitable and necessary for survival".

25

Associated Press, London, UK: September 30, 2024

The leaders of Turkey and India were today both reported victims of attacks similar to other world leaders in previous months. As before, white backpacks were found by the bodies containing notes. India's note said, "The Hindu religion is not a weapon," and Turkey's said, "The games are over."

Neither country has any information about who was responsible for these acts.

26

Herstel released a communique to the leaders of Israel, Afghanistan, China, Saudi Arabia, Turkey, and Myanmar

"The future is set. It will unfold with or without you and your people. This future is peaceful and blanketed in freedom. The choice is yours. Release your people and nurture them for the future or condemn yourself and them to oblivion. They will be aware of your choice. Conduct yourself with honour."

27

With both candidates of the major parties failing to secure the minimum requirement of 270 electoral votes to achieve victory, the congressional majority exercised its responsibility to decide who will be president. The re-election of a former president and the demise of the challenger threw the country into chaos, and disaster ruled the day. Republicans versus Democrats. Black versus white. Rich versus poor. The educated elite versus the not so. The influx of immigrants across the Mexican border became a moot point as vast numbers of white, elite Americans streamed into Canada.

The Canadians, unprepared for such an influx, were caught between a rock and a hard place. The border breaches were pan-continental—east coast to west coast—and while the isolationist provincial Conservative government of Alberta was reluctant to say no to their southern neighbours, the residents of the east and west coasts were not so welcoming. It was easy to offer solutions to global problems from the comfort of a safe haven. However, when your nest is invaded, it is a different matter. Immigrants refugees and uninvited guests were all the same: they needed to be fed and sheltered.

The Conservative government of Canada was unable to rationalize head versus heart, and while it attempted to find answers to the situation spiralled out of control. The global refugee crisis took on a different shade.

Herstel, just prior to the inauguration of the new American president urged all to relax, be humane and compassionate, and accept everyone to the best of their ability and resources. This, he pointed out, should be done globally for all refugees. "What is the worst-case scenario? Not enough resources? This is not the reality, he challenged the Governments.

"It's a question of delivery. Has this not been the case throughout our history everywhere when a few want more than others? Sharing is the better concept and should be tried. It's Mighty Blue and you. You can rule the day. If we stop trying to push each other off the bridge and offer a helping hand instead, we stand a chance of getting to the other side."

The refugee problem began a metamorphosis. It was no longer referred to as a problem. Just life unfolding as it should. It donned a positive cloak.

28

Mali: January 6, 2025

Herstel issued a communique to America.

"I represent humanity. I represent life. There is good. There is bad. We forge a positive course. It will be choppy but humanity, will prevail. This chaos has been a long time in the making. It will take a long time to put the pieces back. Ironically, there will be a positive shift to common sense, and the truth is that the majority of people in the world are already beating the path toward change. When the fighting and hand wringing are over, the inevitable path forward will emerge.

"MLK and Gandhi left us with words. They were only allowed to scratch the surface. Now those words adorn yoga studios. Irony or oxymoron. What I'm saying is change is necessary. It's inevitable. We can no longer pay lip service to the welfare of the world's majority at the expense of the excesses of the lucky few. Wake up! Wisen up. You can take charge of your destiny. It's your free will. And you have begun to do so. The sun is rising on Mighty Blue - and on all of us.

29

During the six months that had passed since the appearance of Herstel and the revelation of the Doctrine of Recovery, the presenter of the hard-hitting interview program No Hiding Place had been transformed, as had the program. It was now a marketplace for the activities relating to the doctrine and very much the troubadour of the Mighty Blue.

At the production meeting for the interview of the United Nations secretary general, Robert was keen to ensure he had every conceivable statistic relating to global change brought about by the Doctrine of Recovery, at least for those elements that were to date embraced by a largely grateful world.

The interview format was now one of sharing as opposed to confrontation. The production team was inundated with requests to appear from individuals in all walks of life who wished to share the progress of the changes. They and No Hiding Place were singing off the same page.

30

Beta: Why lunch? Not on a diet anymore?

Alpha: Kind of. Just wanted some more time as I'm really interested in what Herstel said at the UN yesterday

Beta: So is the entire Universe it seems. It was a clarion call to Mighty Blue. A surge of millions of new registrations creating an air of expectation and excitement. The Blue Wave is building.

Alpha: Have you been dating lately?

Beta: Dating? Going retro. Increasing my venues of activity at a casual pace. You know - gentle stalking. Ha Ha. Avoiding the ultra-needy.

But no luck. I'm too focused on personal goals. I'm not signed on to be a therapist or friend or soul mate. Not interested in fitting into the identikit of someone's dream. Especially if they have no rational reason for the qualities they seek. Most should just get a dog, and some do. Which leaves me falling short of the bar. You know, I'm interested as an observer. For now, it's spectator sport.

Alpha: Well I've competed. It's been five years since I divorced, and that took some years of my life. I'm still looking to get involved if it happens.

Let's say I'm on the bench and ready if the coach calls me up. How was your trip to New York?

Beta: You know everyone there is acting like it's still the center of the universe. They have no idea what's going on with the rest of the world. Do you remember seeing those videos of people on the beach admiring the waves when the tsunami of 2010 happened? At some point they realized they had to run but it was too late. I don't think America has even noticed the current tsunami of social and financial change. I was in a coffee shop, observing as I do, and a couple of young girls - early twenties I think- were arguing where Canada was located. America or Europe "because they speak French there, Dude." No, I didn't intervene. They didn't even think of googling. I guess although there were libraries around for hundreds of years, a large sector humanity never made use of them. Hit me up. What have you got? The veggie bowls here are so good btw.

Alpha: Thanks but I feel like a steak today. So, I have the Doctrine here and I thought we could dissect each element, objectively. I think we are on the verge of something. Not sure what. But, as they would have said in the sixties, "It's a happening." Herstel laid out twenty commandments if I may be so bold. Are you game?

Beta: You bet. This is interesting. You lead, I'll follow.

Alpha: Let's review where we are now relative to the areas Herstel's Doctrine covers.

1. Half the planet are starving, and the other half are killing themselves pursuing material possessions in excess of their needs.
2. We have an excess of guns and military capability and there are wars everywhere.
3. We lack leadership with integrity and purpose.
4. Crime and criminal activities are rampant and unmanageable. Police forces are corrupt and are not trusted.
5. The entertainment and sport industries are without ethics and integrity and are unpalatable

6. Religions rather than be helpful, they typically assist oppression, discrimination and conflict and do not stand up to intellectual scrutiny.
7. Higher education has lost its bearings- its north star.
8. Racism is a growing crutch for many who can't face each day and its challenges with honesty.
9. Consumerism is the only growth industry, driven by fear and greed.
10. The environment is plunging down a well.
11. There is no light at the end of the tunnel.
12. We are ruled by desperate men.
13. We are existing in every possible manner opposite to the UN declaration of Human Rights)and other noble mandates.

"Now let me be clear these are not my views of our current status. They come from those those leaning on the left of the political spectrum. I've presented it this way to give you an on ramp to responses and I leave the gate open to my role as a Devil's advocate. I wouldn't lie to you, but I find what is being proposed in the Doctrine rather concerning, if I may be serious for a moment. The more I think about it – my knee jerk reaction is that it threatens the very existence I occupy and am comfortable with. It's not perfect I know. But change and the unknown are not things most of us are capable of dealing with in a rational manner.

Fear rushes in and we panic. And then it gets ugly. We become selfish and possessive of the things and people - in that order- that we value. And we will fight to the death. It's called survival. And when there are a group of us who feel the same, we become even stronger. I hope that doesn't put you off your veggie-bowl, but I wanted to let you know what's tapping me on the shoulder as I stand and watch the clouds. Some people are seeing silver linings. I am seeing more dark clouds gathering and getting bigger.

Beta: I guess The Doctrine is in the dock and I'm Defence Attorney. Who Ho! Law and Order rules. Now to begin we must try and keep in mind some fundamental principles which underpin Herstel's philosophy for change:

Humanity as a collective has allowed itself to be oppressed, servile and led by fear. The voices of the many shining individuals who have cried out against our negative traits taking charge, have been lost in the wind. The collective, led by individual action must now concentrate on our positive traits. And that affects everything we can think of, in our daily lives, in our broader existence and in the lives of future generations.

I wonder what would change if we focused on, rewarded and valued the impact of our work over the status achieved?

I wonder what would happen if we were allowed to follow our better instincts and take care of ourselves, our soul and our spirituality; if we treated others with kindness. If that could happen, we would always be in the sun.

Where do we begin?

Alpha: The very first proposal "Eradicate poverty and hunger". I see what he's looking to do. Or to be more accurate, what he is expecting to be done. Not clear by whom. But the biggest question relates to money. It always comes down to money doesn't it? The numbers are all sexy and persuade that it's a simple supply and demand exercise. But it's going to cost a shit load of money, my friend. Where does it all come from? Second question while it's in my mind. These are just proposals, right? I mean the entire Doctrine. Herstel doesn't have any legal, financial, political or military standing. He's no more than a pop star or a Hollywood star with a micro phone. Even if he had official status, his goals are impossible to achieve unless there is a seismic shift in the way humanity functions. And that means pretty much everyone would have to be on board. How will these - and I'll call them suggestions - be implemented?

Beta: There! You have it in a nutshell! But I'll come back to that general question later.

First, let's look at poverty and hunger. So, the premise is sound. There is enough food and raw materials to ensure everyone can avoid chronic hunger, shelter safely and obtain basic health care. The first challenge is finding the supplies and making them available to those in need.

The second is identifying those in need and providing them with the means to purchase what they need. So, we have a delivery logistic and an identification exercise. The latter is being – and I say being as this started on the day of - Here Comes the Sun and the opening of the Olympics in April - managed by AI who have access to all existing government and public data available.

Delivery and identification will not be perfect at the outset, but the system will self-correct with all new data received when in operational mode. There are numerous turnstiles imbedded in the system to prevent criminal activity and fraud. The global aid networks – civilian and government – are being re-organised and efficiently managed to access and deliver supplies to those in need.

These operations are, I understand, being governed by the various Mighty Blue groups who have seemingly endless resources, and access to everything they need to succeed.

With regards to the money, all I can ascertain is this. Herstel has not addressed money directly but has alluded to possibilities. I'll get into that when we talk about reparations. Suffice to say there is money to accomplish all activities proposed. He has teasingly said, with a broad smile, "We will be like thieves in the night."

Now your second question. How am I doing so far? Not alleviating your fears, am I?

Alpha: Before we go on, let's order. How much do you know about this as a whole? Was your visit to New York related to Herstel?

The waiter is patient and smiles. Gentlemen?

Beta: Spaghetti Linguine for me, please.

Alpha: Describe your house burger for me.

The waiter obliges and Alpha listens intently, pauses and surveys the ceiling.

OK, I'll have your burger and a glass of your house red.

Beta: New York. Full Disclosure. I registered on Mighty Blue in March and re-imagined my life. Immediately I felt I had shaken off all of the unnecessary aspects of my life and was able to relax and focus on those aspects which are important to me. I've shifted into a service mindset and have stopped thinking about financial needs and aspirations. I'm imbedded with Mighty Blue as much as I desire. It feels like a dream. It's difficult to explain.

Alpha: Sounds like you've joined a cult, my man.

Beta: Ha! I recently read a book titled Return Empty to Paradise which is a coming of age story set in the sixties. In it the hero, Sunny, describes stepping out onto the street one morning when he was 10 years old, accompanied by his father and uncle who they were visiting. His uncle lived in a small village in Guyana which looked out onto the Atlantic Ocean.

Everywhere they went they were greeted with smiles, pats on the back. Friendly insults and jokes were accompanied by raucous and hearty laughter. It was a sunny morning and Sunny felt safe and wrapped in joy and happiness, without a care in the world. That's how I feel.

I was invited to join a group of registrants like myself who are effectively gatekeepers, monitoring the progress of the Doctrine. I must admit we have access to some spectacular software to help us out. I'm hoping I can meet Herstel sometime in the future, as he is very interested in our work.

Alpha: I take it then you know more than the average joe about what is real and what is wishful thinking.

Beta: In a sense. Now the second aspect regarding logistics, to keep us on track. Since the announcements at the Olympics a number of suggestions as you call them have begun to take shape. A lot of what is happening is being done quietly and quickly. There appears to be a reluctance by the regular media to go digging for "breaking news."

It's happening and because the cause and effect is so all encompassing it's difficult to report on the overall picture. Plus, those involved are just happily getting on with their lives , and have no interest in publicity. Add to the mix, many in the media are themselves "in the cult" and would prefer to allow change to evolve unimpeded, without obstruction.

Also important is the fact that these changes are driven by the individual primarily and then by the collective thereafter. So, there are events occurring which may appear related but are not directly connected. For example, the leadership in Russia, China, Israel, Saudi Arabia and Afghanistan have changed this year. All in mysterious circumstances.

Alpha: Also, Turkey, Iran and India.

Beta: What is very surprising is the lack of an uprising in support of the incumbent, in any of those countries. Equally surprising, known supporters and followers of the departed leaders have not rushed to fill the void. Strong men are feeling vulnerable. What's next?

Alpha: Oh, an easy one. "Remove the mask of racism,"

Beta: We've toyed with this before.

Alpha: Yes, I think we agreed you can't remove racism with legislation.

Beta: Racism is about fear, tribalism and honesty. We've been hard wired with the former two and are quite often reluctant to make good use of the latter. But there is no magic pill here. This will change with a wave of awareness as each and every one courageously stares into the mirror. This is where the collective will be most helpful and effective: just one global Alcohol Anonymous style meeting every hour every day. It will all come to pass and when it does, we will look back at current perceptions, practices and divisions as just plain stupid.

Alpha: Hmmm. Well, I'll come along for the ride as you know quite a few of my friends are of ethnic backgrounds. But for some of the population it might get complicated. Honesty is a difficult pill to swallow. You heard about the guy who insists he's non-violent. He was happy to beat you up if you didn't believe him.

Beta: Ha ha. I think for you a little more than hitching a ride will be needed.

Alpha: Dem's fightin' words, pardner! Anyway, let's move on. Next is re-duction of civilian gun ownership. I assume the US of A with their cherished "right to bear arms" will not be part of this. So, enlighten me.

Beta: You are right. There are three groups it appears. The USA, the rest of the developed world and the less developed countries who are home to the majority of terrorists' groups and rebel armies.

In America, those who are strongly against giving up their arms want to be prepared when the government comes after them. I guess they have ignored the fact that America has the mightiest military on the planet. They will be taking a stick to a gunfight. Any way I understand that whilst the majority of the world will be embracing the doctrine and changing direction,

America will be standing on the sidelines engaged in a knockdown family fight. When that is done, what's left of the "greatest country on earth" will dust themselves off and play catch up. For the other groups money for arms trade will be hugely successful, but only for a while.

With a positive shift out of poverty and gainful opportunities available via Mighty Blue, new recruits will be harder to find. Couple that with the strangling of money supply to terrorist groups and rebel armies, retaining existing members will become impossible. The chance to live a normal life with economic opportunities will rescue members of these organisations who had previously had no choice. The same will apply to crime organisations who will grow weak as their assets disappear and their activities will falter from lack of resources and dwindling membership. Potential members will find the grass is greener elsewhere.

It is expected that the old model of a small group of the recalcitrant controlling by force will not work as the collective becomes more aware and supportive of each other. They will be a powerful force in communities, neighbourhoods, towns and villages.

Time and money are the key elements here. But the time is nigh.

Alpha: ok. I put this in the category of pure speculation. You've simplified a complex problem. But hey, who knows? Can't wait to see when that gets going.

Now Reverse climate change. They've been banging this drum for decades and a significant part of the population doesn't even believe in climate change. Don't know what they believe in. Reminds me of a Marx Brothers movie in which Chico says to someone he's trying to win over, "Are you going to believe your own eyes, or what I tell you?" So, what's going to change here?

Beta: This is simply about setting free and harnessing the solutions without delay. Some facts: The oil industry has been aware of climate change for over 40 years. They conducted experiments to confirm their observations and then set about spreading misinformation, denying climate change. As it did with the tobacco industry, this tactic worked to delay positive global solutions. There are a variety of technological and natural solutions available that when harnessed together can reverse climate change. We simply need everyone on board, pulling together in the same direction.

And the greatest of all enforcers, Nature, will quicken the call to action. Most importantly the major obstacle to dealing with climate change, the politicians – will now collectively make this their priority. Which leads us nicely to the next topic.

Alpha: Hold politicians legally responsible. I see. We would certainly all love to do that. But how?

Beta: Well, politicians are the only profession who are not prosecuted for negligence, incompetence or wrongdoing. If we allowed doctors or engineers the same degree of freedom, it would be a more dangerous world. Politics attracts opportunists more than idealists. Supreme courts globally will be petitioned to enact laws which hold politicians to fulfil their manifestos

bar exceptional circumstances.

They will be mandated to serve the people in their actions and policies. It will be illegal for them to favour special interests groups and to profit from their position. Incumbents will be given two years to re-set their course after which the new laws will come into effect. Aspiring participants will be held accountable from the outset.

Alpha: Now that's a Hail Mary if I ever heard one. The existing miscreants will have to propose laws which in effect will potentially send them to jail. How on earth will that happen?

Beta: Power of the people. Power of the people.

Alpha: I'm going to put that in the category of naïve.

Next reparations. Who? When? And How? Those are questions regarding both money and laws.

Beta: This I know has begun and is deep and wide ranging. I was privileged to learn about the progress when I was in New York. Groups of lawyers globally have taken on the task of identifying those laws in their jurisdiction which have proven to be roadblocks to the natural progress of slaves and indentured labourers in their home countries and abroad.

They will set about having these laws changed. At the same time financial analysts are creating a global map of communities which have suffered from the effect, past and present of, slavery. They will determine how best these communities can be helped to bridge the gap created, and also the cost of the repair.

Those corporations and private estates which have benefited from the exploitation of slaves over several generations will have their assets redirected to meet the demands of reparations.

Alpha: Is this a Robin Hood operation or will the beneficiaries be requested to contribute? I can't see many admitting liabilities or wanting to hand over some or all of their assets.

Beta: There will be no requests, as far as I know. What is needed will be taken. Much like the colonialists took what they wanted, without any questions.

Alpha: Touché. But there is going to be trouble.

Beta: Many will feel wronged but how will the world react? That will be interesting and the key. Sometimes logic, rational thinking and fairness are viewed differently depending on your interests. When the Israelis kicked the Palestinians out of their homes, stole their land and made them a nation of prisoners with no future you would have thought that the world would have stood up and said no. But sometimes logic does not prevail and the wronged are left helpless. This exercise is vast and complex and affects over 70 per cent of the world's population. It won't go unnoticed for long. Keep a close watch on your bank account.

Beta is convulsed with laughter. Alpha is not amused as he ponders the possibilities.

Beta: Don't worry about your money. You have lots. What's next?

Alpha: Eradicate modern slavery. Oh wait. What about that Palestinian issue? Surely, that needs to be resolved.

Beta: Well Herstel doesn't spend much time on this. His take is that this is not a logistical problem. The problem is the story told: The story needs to change. It's a matter of time, but the time is soon. If it's an eye for an eye, whose eyes? Sooner or later everyone is blind. Sooner or later they return to the land, dust to dust. Here's what I think will happen:

All aid to Israel is intercepted- happens for a while before it's realised by Israeli as it is intercepted by Mighty Blue and re-directed to Palestinians. As this comes to pass, the USA will not have the will or resources to continue with supplies. Dialogue will replace arms.

The holocaust was the premier demonstration of racism and colonialism in its execution and its aftermath in that the exterminated races deemed inferior were of less or little importance.

Alpha: Well that was easy. Kissinger must be spinning.... . Back to modern slavery?

Beta: Ah, this is one of the easiest or so it would appear. And AI plays a large part. The global supply and demand network is analysed to identify those at the top of the chain - the buyers - and those at the bottom- the workers. Assets of the buyers such as mining companies and retail corporations will be appropriated to provide acceptable working conditions and wages for workers. The concept of endless growth will need to be addressed by all corporations.

Alpha: That sounds good and noble, but it means the cost of living in developed countries will go through the roof. A lot of companies will go under.

Beta: That's a certainty. Especially vulnerable are those companies who, with the help of the banks, exist on massive annual losses. Now if you went to your bank and told them that you are functional and doing well, but you are going to need an overdraft which will increase annually - and your bank says yes. You would be very happy. You can then go about your merry way buying and acquiring as you wish.

Yes, there will be causalities in the war of correction, as there were when the Doctrine of Discovery kicked in . And that has continued - the causalities I mean – to this day.

Alpha: I have to admit this all sounds crazy and dangerous and I feel threatened personally if all or some of this becomes real. But at the same time, I'm beginning to feel like I want to be part of your cult.

Beta: That's interesting. Let's keep going.

Alpha: Limit inherited wealth. Is this a dig at Royal families? There are not many of those left.

Beta: Most Royal families have substantial assets passed down over generations, the acquisition of which would now be viewed as dubious. In addition, they are also receiving handsome income from the state. The proposal is that incumbents retain the status quo but when they pass the majority of their estate goes to the state into a public fund for future emergency use.

The total worth of billionaires – remember just billionaires- is around twelve trillion dollars. Over the next twenty years five trillion will pass over to their heirs at 150 billion per year. Inheritance will be limited, with the balance being held in a public fund. The success of corporations depends on the people who work for them and those who buy their products. It could be argued that the profits belong to the public more so than children who like royalty are beneficiaries through accident of birth.

Alpha: I'll buy that. I think everyone should work for what they have. People need to work. They need to contribute positively. They needs to do something of value. The problem with the younger generation is they seem to lack goals and are not focused. Everyone wants to be rich and famous. Now you can be rich and famous without offering anything of substance. Kids coming out of college are qualified but not smart. They are missing something. Now listen to me the old man.

Beta: You are right. When you turn sixteen you take a driving test to be licensed to drive a car - a lethal weapon. But you don't have to prove you know anything about car maintenance or how it works. That's a vital part that's missing. Taking that to the extreme, any idiot or pair of idiots can become parents. Why? Most young or even not so young people you know you wouldn't hire because they lack relevant skills for the workplace.

Yet these people can have unsupervised responsibility for the welfare of a child. This problem is not mentioned in the Doctrine but is on Mighty Blue which calls for the creation and deployment of a global youth force who will spend two years, ages eighteen to twenty, working in communities across the globe. It will shape them and teach them the value of working together, service and self-discipline.

Alpha: That's a winner. Pre-college I take it. Every parent will be on board.

Beta: How are we doing for time? Is the Professor still feeling threatened?

Alpha: Actually, I'm now in the zone of confusion.

Next is sharing corporate profits with all workers. I don't think we need to go into that. It's kinda covered by some of what we've gone through already. Any way it's an oxymoron.

Now aid. That's such a mess. What will happen there?

Beta: The road to hell is paved with good intentions. The aid ecosystem is populated with people who are genuinely concerned about those in need and want to help but the entire system is dysfunctional and unable to deliver. One percent of aid actually gets to those in need. The money is largely used to pay for the millions of jobs which are created in the developed countries.

The system will function positively when those with good intentions are allowed to act positively and the administrative positions are largely held in the localities where the aid is needed. The funds will be managed by AI assistance which will ensure a more efficient delivery. Also, with some of the other changes taking shape there will be a huge knock on effect.

So for example, with the reduction of poverty and payment of reparations in progress the need for aid will lessen. One major are is that Governments will no longer be allowed to lend vast sums of money to less developed countries with the proviso that most of the money is used to buy arms from the lender. This is what has been branded as aid in the past.

Alpha: Why will governments agree to that? It's a huge source of income for them.

Beta: Well, let's jump to one of the items further ahead on your list, the reduction of national military stockpiles. The primary responsibility of the government is to protect its people. The state should not be the most important player. Who or what is the state? This model only breeds power and corruption. Most countries have never used their military capabilities, so why fund it?

It's just a huge waste of money. Those countries that have made use of their military have unilaterally done so to the detriment of the innocent and the weak whose fate would have been no different if they had no military capabilities. The money spent annually on defence budgets can best be used elsewhere, for the benefit of humanity.

Large military capabilities only encourage dictators to practice mischief. The ideal solution and this will take time – is the establishment of a global peace force well equipped and of sufficient numbers to be deployed rapidly to eradicate any action which demonstrates deliberate intent to harm any section of humanity. We are human and sometimes we cannot help straying into the dark side. There I sound like Herstel.

Mighty Blue demonstrated on September 14th that there exists out there – and no end of investigation has been unable to determine where or what – the power to disable all military systems. It must now have occurred to war mongers that any future military engagement could be completely out of their control. Therefore, that would seem to be a path not worth pursuing. We hope.

Alpha: Again, this is a dream. Who will be responsible for creating and deploying such a force? The impossible obstacle is vested interests. No one wants to be vulnerable. The perfect example of that model being unworkable is the United Nations Security Council. It's a completely useless organisation because everyone's singing off a different page and no one is prepared to admit it doesn't work.

Beta: that's right. But it is expected that with the re-making of the political, social and economic landscapes, the general approach to such challenges will be accomplished by greater cooperation with integrity and candour to achieve a common goal. Remember, humanity is shifting gear and direction.

Alpha: I was toying with the idea of re-imagining myself but when I looked at what is being asked of me - an honest and comprehensive review of my life- it's not simple or easy. In fact, its a bit scary. It's like taking a cold plunge. Your advice would be to "just jump in!"

I don't know if you realise it, but you are a very passionate advocate for the Doctrine. Does anyone know where Herstel is and how to contact him?

With all of the poverty and aid changes in play not to mention the reparations and taking out the world's military capability, the world and their dogs must be looking for him. He's making the world's intel look pretty toothless. The media seem to have taken a passive position. They wait to hear from him. That's wild. Do you have his cell number? Alpha asks cagily.

Beta: Don't need it. He's staying at my place. Don't tell anyone.

Beta is very amused as Alpha laughs nervously and makes a quick mental note to stalk Beta's place of abode. "What's left of the Doctrine? I think we can power through as the major items have all been looked at."

Alpha: Well, well, well. The Abolition of organised religion is not major? I think you've left the planet. What about this? I can't wrap my head around how billions of people will get through the day without this drug. I can see the benefit of dismantling the material side of religions and their practices but how are people going to deal without their religious support or belief?

Beta: I think you are talking about two different things here: religion and spirituality. People need to connect to their spirituality. There is spiritualty in religion but there is no religion in spirituality. I see it as a personal journey. I think lots of people will be freed from the shackles of organised practices. Organised religion is a menace to society. How do you feel about that?

Alpha: Actually, the more I think about it ,I should spend more time exploring my spiritually. The rest of it is mostly community activities. It just gives one the sense of belonging, but it diminishes your desire to be curious. A lot of the "stories" are porous and do require a great deal of faith. They falter when exposed to intellectual scrutiny. I'll leave that there for the moment.

Beta: Word is The Pope will lead the change by resigning his position and offering guidance for the Catholic church to make the transition. I don't think that's from Herstel. Just leaks coming from the Vatican. Early directives have already gone out to the Cardinals to prepare them for the change.

Alpha: That is a huge shift for humanity. Now what about the refugees which a major global problem?

Beta: This is one of those areas which will benefit from the other changes we discussed. Refugees are economic or political. Most people, all things considered would prefer to stay in their homeland if they are safe and can prosper there. There will soon be a reverse journey for refugees everywhere as they become aware of the changes.

Alpha: Now that may be a real problem for developed countries with low birthrates who need the population growth. That would be ironic. What do they say? Be careful you what you wish for.

Beta: Who are these people that say that? He chuckles. How was your burger?

Alpha: It was good. Not the best. That reminds me about the global shift to a plant-based diet. I think that is inevitable and will be rapid when supply drives demand. Fundamentally, we have to eat. But we don't have to eat other living creatures. People need educating about the horrors of the meat industry and its spectacular inefficiency and detriment to the planet. There's no bigger meat eater than me as you know but I have to admit I have been eating veggie burgers lately, by choice. It's just food. We will eat what is available. Choice is a first world problem. Our consumption is off the scale.

I met a guy in Barbados a few years ago who was the picture of health. A local taxi driver who from had retired from a government post earlier and was driving a cab to stay busy. He looked twenty years younger than his age. "I don't touch dairy or meat" he said. " You know humankind is the only specie who insists on drinking milk after the weaning age. In fact, they are drinking the milk produced by animals for their young. Now we know a mother's milk is naturally created for her offspring. It's not meant for consumption of others. You know what I mean?"

I didn't really get into what he meant but I had a sense of where he was going with that. I didn't eat eggs for quite a while after that.

Beta: Are you going to miss those homemade milk shakes?

Alpha: I already do. I think we are nearly done. Let's see; Realistic income for sports stars and movie stars. You don't need to explain that to me. How the hell did we get to a place where a guy is paid a million a week to kick a ball around. These are full time jobs that people do by choice.

They should be paid on a sensible scale. I love football and the movies but I'm not going to suffer if I don't see another movie or football match. However, if my boiler breaks down in the winter or I have a heart attack I will make a good case for paying any doctor or plumber a million dollars. We need to get real.

Beta: What about the illegal production and distribution of drugs? These are not recreational but prescription drugs. The intent is to identify and terminate the illegal supply sources which will impact the distribution networks. This seems like a tough one but Herstel had alluded to "the angels of mercy" having a hand in this. I must admit I don't know much else about it.

And finally, a global force to deal with natural disasters.

Alpha: That is an absolute necessity and will help to draw the world together.

Beta: You got it! I'm glad we did this. Are you still fearful?

Alpha: No. Now I'm intrigued. I'm going to re-imagine myself!

Beta: I'm really interested in seeing how you progress.

Alpha: Me, too!

Beta: I'm going to be away for about six months. I've had a request to work with a group in Mali who are working on psychedelic solutions for mental health problems. Its huge issue which needs urgent attention. I know little else about it, just being led by my desire to offer service. Great meeting with you ,as always. Let's do this over WhatsApp while I'm away.

Alpha: For sure. Safe journey and thanks for this. I'm excited.

31

Interview of the United Nations Secretary General, No Hiding Place Studios: December 2025

Following the appearance of Herstel at the United Nations General Assembly, the leadership of the United Nations changed hands. The new Secretary General - a long time employee of the organization at various levels - was adamant his aim was to embrace, as closely and as quickly as possible, the elements of the Doctrine of Recovery.

Robert: Good morning, Secretary General. Thank you for taking the time from your busy schedule to be with us. We're interested in a mid-term report, so to speak, of your new position and your overview of what has transpired since you took the reins of your organization some fifteen months ago. And here, let me help you with some facts which my team has gathered.

The majority of those who were suffering from poverty in the developed and less developed world now have some financial means to control their daily lives.

The global aid infrastructure has been to some extent dismantled and rebuilt by those who work in that sector.

Military aid has disappeared.

The ownership of personal firearms is now viewed negatively, and the aim is to gather and destroy as many guns as possible.

The pope and heads of most organised religions have resigned and handed over their responsibilities to management groups with secular goals.

The view of nationalism is changing. What is the point of borders? Many people are now moving to cultural identity as more important.

In politics, accountability is driven by civic groups, which has changed the nature of politics and the calibre of people entering civil and community service.

The financial model of all major sports has changed drastically to eliminate the mega earnings of the past.

There appears to be a shift on racism as people look to themselves as opposed to looking for scapegoats to blame for their personal failures or shortcomings.

Refugees have reduced dramatically in numbers and are now easily accepted in most countries.

And of course, the removal or demise—whatever you wish to call it—of leaders or leading members of dictatorships has been transformative for those countries and their citizens.

And of course, war or the threat of it. Those in the military are now convinced that warfare is not sustainable given the vulnerability of all weaponry to whatever power Herstel and his people possess.

The Mighty Blue has almost 3 billion registrants and is growing by 100 million every two weeks.

So, where would you like to begin?

Secretary General: That would be a good place to begin.

Robert: Has this personal shift on a personal level of those registrants been largely responsible for the changes you mentioned?

Secretary General: Everything you mentioned has been possible due to the individual workers in all organizations finding purpose and the freedom to execute their duties in a productive and positive manner. Dysfunction and waste are being rooted out everywhere. The support of Mighty Blue has a lot to do with the success we're experiencing. There has been a complete shift in the mindset of the workforce. It's remarkable. We've moved from the mindset that every problem is impossible to deal with, to all problems have solutions.

The Secretary General continued to explain in detail the transformation of his agency and also those organizations it interfaced with.

Secretary General: The future has never looked so promising, Robert. If you give people independence, they will thrive.

32

THE EMBRACEMENT

February 2026

In the fifteen months following Herstel's address to the United Nations General Assembly, he was rarely seen. He made no more speeches nor appearances in the media. Brief glimpses of him in those parts of the world where the impact of poverty and hunger relief were being felt showed him connecting with the people. These were powerful images. He was also seen in those countries whose leaders of dictatorial and repressive regimes were no longer in charge. The freedom and exhilaration felt by the people in these places swept away the aspirations dictatorial wannabees may have had about trying to fill the void.

Generally, people sought to pursue lives devoid of drama, and they were aided by the skillful civil service class, who took the reins of management and offered leadership devoid of toxic politics.

Certainly, they had a purpose.

Now life was in the hands of the people, not the state.

In the background, the presence of Mighty Blue, with its infinite resources, gave everyone the comfort to pursue lives of meaning and purpose. The Backpackers, as the press labelled them, also with good cause, were prominent in everyone's memory. Fear was being relegated to the back seat.

There were of course those who clung, without rhyme or reason, to the dysfunctional practices of the past. They were for the most part allowed to function as they saw fit. Increasingly, it became apparent to them that their future was located in a cul-de-sac.

The majority choose not to engage or confront these resistors, as they christened themselves, so there was no fuel to drive their vehicle. For the most part, they held each other up like drunks in the night.

The criminal element found it increasingly difficult to operate. Where the general population had been previously ruled by gang warfare, it was now emboldened and defended itself as a collective. Street crime everywhere was dramatically reduced as local neighbourhoods became community conscious and looked out for each other. It just seemed a more rewarding and positive way to exist. With the resources available through Mighty Blue, many gang members and potential recruits found more rewarding avenues and activities to pursue. The financial resources of these criminal organizations were sourced and drained, and normal operations became impossible. Survival was becoming the main concern for those who wished to continue such activities. The burning question was how?

Rumours, which were not substantiated, were that the Backpackers had put the leaders of the major crime organizations on notice. Whether this was true or not was irrelevant, as the rumour itself was self-serving.

No longer rushing aimlessly in pursuit of the intangibles and the unnecessary, people found time to breathe ,and to take care of themselves and one another.

The great puzzle, which was now becoming folklore, as those whose lives were impacted positively didn't really care, was the source of funds that fueled the reparations and the peel back of poverty.

Mighty Blue Financial was now, by sheer volume of activity, the largest bank in the world. Its digital currency fast becoming a contender for the global currency title.

This heralded problems for the American economy, overburdened with debt and adding more fuel to the fires raging born of division and cynical corruption in that country. Refusing to let go of their Greatest Country on Earth banner and play ball with the rest of the world, they, like previous empires, were rushing blindly into oblivion.

"They will return and take up important global leadership," said Herstel. "But first, they will burn the house down. They will be led by those who contributed vastly in the growth of the republic. Those who by default were honed at the anvil in the process of surviving, producing the fittest and sharpest of survivors. The Afro-Americans and Indigenous peoples will readily take the reins."

The news media's penchant for drama was fading as consumers were finding less interest. Also in decline were the negative elements of social media. People were choosing to interact with each other or with nature as a more enjoyable and rewarding course.

The leading social media site, which ironically was created by someone who found it difficult to interact with people and succeeded in isolating millions from meaningful social interaction, was fast imploding. It was a sign of the times. More purposeful sites were evolving.

The dissolution of organized religion was the biggest challenge for most. In the developed world, finding alternative employment for the clergy was the immediate need but most segued to providing consulting services to those who chose to continue with religious practices. These were, of course, in the minority in developed countries.

In the least developed countries, the transition away from religion was proving more difficult and would almost certainly require a generational change. In the interim, communities were alerted to be aware of those seeking to exploit the vulnerable in this transition. Change is never smooth nor easy.

The opportunity of pursuing gainful employment and peaceful existence for most members of terrorist groups and rebel armies had seriously depleted the ranks of those organizations. Money was always the primary attraction for young recruits who had no alternative opportunities. Funds for these organizations were also drying up, as was the supply of firearms, as global production was significantly reduced.

With the exception of America, the rest of the world embraced the notion of discarding firearms for civilians use, and government purchase from owners quickened the process.

With the introduction of white hydrogen and several other new developments, the reversal of climate change was gathering pace.

The arc of human progress in peace and prosperity was bent upward.

33

BBC Studios: Question Time February 2025

On the anniversary of Herstel Fidia's very first appearance in public, a show on BBC TV presented a special to explore the changes that were being experienced during the Blue Wave, as the period was now commonly referred to in the fashion of the Swinging Sixties or Roaring Twenties.

The presenter, dressed in Royal Blue, welcomed the audience. "On this very day one year ago, in this very studio, Herstel Fidia - he places his right palm over his heart, which has become a common gesture whenever Herstel is mentioned - appeared to an unsuspecting world.

Very soon after, the world began to learn of Mighty Blue, and what followed is commonly referred to as the Blue Wave, which has affected us all in some form or other.

Herstel—and I stress we know little of this person except his ability to disappear and then show up on the other side of the planet without ever any adequate notice—over a period of nine months described a series of initiatives designed to put humanity on a positive course.

Where is he now? No one knows. But that is somewhat irrelevant, as our world is wrapped in a warm blanket of positive change. It seems that at last John Lennon's plea is being heard: Give peace a chance. He was also partially right that, love is all we need.

What wasn't clear, and still isn't to some extent, is who or what was implementing these changes. Whatever the answer, changes are real and have gripped a large part of our human family. We will summarize briefly the changes that occurred - if at all any - in the areas Herstel addressed.

Poverty

Racism

Climate change (hydrogen; plant-based diet)

Civil gun ownership

Reparations

Modern slavery

Inherited wealth

Political accountably

Aid (civilian and government)

Religion

Refugees

National military stockpile/global force

Gender equality

Mental health care

Nationalism/focus on culture to celebrate diversity. Eradicate meaningless borders.

Sports and entertainment (scale back in rewards to workers in both industries).

Welfare of the individual not the state.

"Let us have your comments and suggestions. We will take responses from our live audience and also from those online.

We will be ending he programme with a live performance of the prophetic Before the Deluge which always offers us the opportunity to reflect.

Let's get started."

FINALLY

MIGHTY BLUE AND YOU – PAUSE TO REFLECT
AND RE-IMAGINE YOURSELF

Mighty Blue – following Hershel's speech (April 2024) – enrolled one million users in 8 hours and twenty million during the week that followed. Within months that number would grow to over 450 million, increasing daily.

HAPPINESS

Money – or, rather, economic security – is important. "We are less happy when we struggle for food security and housing and all that, which is obvious," he says. *What is less obvious is that, above a certain income level, happiness doesn't go up by much, at least according to a 2010 study that set the threshold for US households at $75,000 (£49,000 at that time). The enduring factor is relationships with other people. Waldinger has boiled down his definition of a good life to this: "Being engaged in activities I care about with people I care about."* waldinger/shultz, the good life.

RACISM - will be eroded by personal confrontation of truth.

"You must not lose faith in humanity. Humanity is an ocean; if a few drops of the ocean are dirty, the ocean does not become dirty." gandhi

"A man is but a product of his thoughts. What he thinks he becomes" gandhi

"Life's most persistent and urgent question is, 'What are you doing for others?" dr.ml king

"Whatever affects one directly, affects all indirectly. I can never be what I ought to be until you are what you ought to be. This is the interrelated structure of reality." dr.ml king jr.

"All labor that uplifts humanity has dignity and importance and should be undertaken with painstaking excellence." dr.ml king jr.

"Change does not roll in on the wheels of inevitability but comes through continuous struggle. And so, we must straighten our backs and work for our freedom. A man can't ride you unless your back is bent. "dr.ml king jr.

"If I cannot do great things, I can do small things in a great way." dr.ml king jr.

"Injustice anywhere is a threat to justice everywhere. We are caught in an inescapable network of mutuality, tied in a single garment of destiny. Whatever affects one directly, affects all indirectly." dr.ml king jr.

"The best way to keep a prisoner from escaping is to make sure he never knows he's in prison." dostoevsky.

I have a dream that my four little children will one day live in a nation where they will not be judged by the color of their skin but by the content of their character." dr.ml king jr.

"Here's how great it is to be white: I can get in a time machine and go to any time, and it would be f***ing awesome when I get there! That is exclusively a white privilege." louis ck.

CLIMATE CHANGE

Only when the last tree has died
And the last river been poisoned
And the last fish been caught

Will we realise we cannot eat money.
cree indian proverb

Before the Deluge

Some of you are dreamers
And some of you are fools
Who are making plans and thinking of the future
With the energy of the innocent

Some of you are angry
At the way the earth was abused
By the men who learned how to forge her beauty into power
And they struggled to protect her from them
Only to be confused
By the magnitude of her fury in the final hour
And when the sand is gone and the time arrives
In the naked dawn only a few survive
And in attempts to understand a thing so simple and so huge
Believe that you were meant to live after the deluge

Let creation reveal its secrets by and by, by and by
When the light that's lost within us reaches the sky

Jackson Browne

WAR

Until the philosophy which hold one race
Superior and another inferior
is finally and permanently discredited and abandoned
Everywhere is war, me say war.
That until there are no longer first class
and second class citizens af any nation

Until the color of a man's skin
is of no more significance than the color of his eyes
Me say war.
That until the basic human rights are equally
guaranteed to all, without regard to race
A dis a war.
That until that day
the dream of lasting peace, world citizenship
rule of international morality
will remain in but a fleeting illusion
to be pursued, but never attained
Now everywhere is war, war.
And until the ignoble and unhappy regimes
that hold our brothers in Angola, in Mozambique,
South Africa sub-human bondage
have been toppled, utterly destroyed
Well, everywhere is war, me say war.
War in the east, war in the west
war up north, war down south
war, war, rumours of war.
And until that day, the African continent
will not know peace, we Africans will fight
we find it necessary and we know we shall win
as we are confident in the victory.
Of good over evil, good over evil, good over evil
Good over evil, good over evil, good ever evil.

Bob Marley

Herstel's parting message as appeared on Mighty Blue February 2025

I did my best, it wasn't much
I couldn't feel so I learned to touch
I've told the truth; I didn't come all this way to fool you

so, I'll stand right here before your need for song
With nothing on my tongue but hallelujah
Hallelujah, Hallelujah.

CONCLUSION

Great-grandson: Papa, what do you think would have happened if Herstel didn't show up?

Grandpa: Almost everyone was focused on greed and survival at the expense of others. To the man with a hammer, every problem's a nail. And humanity's hammer was force. As far as records show, humanity was locked in a seemingly endless cycle of violence and exploitation. That would have continued but with greater intensity. The world was on a destructive path of no return. When Herstel showed up I was in my twenties. That was over seventy years ago. The world has changed rapidly in that period. A lot of practices and means of daily existence from that period no longer exist. Humanity and life is constantly evolving. It's just that sometimes the direction it takes is not the best. If I look back seventy years from when I was in my twenties, that would have been in the 1940's and not much from that period was relevant to my early years. Change just marches on.

Great-grandson: So Papa I've been reading lots of history and I have lots of questions. Back in the day when you were twenty one, that was when the Mighty Blue was just forming. Yes? Ha Ha. Just kidding! And a guy called

God was still mostly in charge. What happened to him? He didn't exist in the first place and now he still doesn't exist. So what has changed?

Grandpa: That's going to take a lifetime to explain because a lot of the information about that does not make sense. There is little logic. Next question.

Great-grandson: There were also people called politicians who managed everything. And they were so bad for such a long time. I can't understand how they got the job. Papa, what's iPhone? and cell phone? and mobile phone?

Grandpa: That's how everyone communicated. Calls, video clips, music. Everything really.

Great-grandson: They carried a device around? What would happen if it got lost? Or stolen? They watched lots of TV and played lots of video games. Wasn't that boring? Didn't they like to use their brain?

Grandpa: They didn't have the mind chip that we now use to chat and watch visual images. so we can do that anywhere we want and when we want. we don't have to carry devices around and sit in front of a screen. Also, another thing difficult to explain was that people were treated differently according to color of skin, wealth, education, and social standing. They were judged on meaningless parameters they had no control over.

Now if people are judged at all, it's based on character. There are so many changes. Life practices then were focused on the acquisition of material wealth. Now we treasure service, and connecting to nature, and the spiritual. There was rapid change of mindset when personal goals and practices were changed. When people became free of harmful practices and pursuits, when they were free of insecurity and fear - social and economic - happiness swept in like a tsunami.

Great-grandson: You'll have to explain that a bit more for me. So much of the past doesn't make sense. Mighty Blue was divided into different areas called countries, right? And the countries fought each other. What for?

Grandpa: That is hard to understand. Lots of guns were owned by lots of people, so lots of people were killed.

Great-grandson: There must have been a lot of danger everywhere, right?

Grandpa: There was little value placed on the lives of many who unfortunately paid the price for the greed and excesses of a minority. Entire generations only knew danger. One big change was diet which resulted in healthier humans and helped Mighty Blue to regenerate its resources.

Great-grandson: I guess what we have is called a plant-based diet because in the past you ate animals. Yeah, eating animals. That's crazy. You had to kill them, right? How do you kill a cow? They are so big. Did you eat a whole cow? And chickens would have to be caught? Did you eat the feathers too? And fishes. OMG. Whales-there are bigger than houses. My head's exploding. There was something called a hot dog. Did they eat dogs?

Grandpa: No, but don't ask. Are you hungry?

Great-grandson: Yes, I could eat a horse. Ha ha. Now I know what that expression means. Oh! One more thing I don't understand. Way back in history people were always in different classes. Like plebs and patricians. Was that like judging people for no real reason?

Grandpa : So plebs were people who didn't have a lot a value - common people they were called. And patricians were aristocrats who were in charge. On top. A bit like politicians. And royalty. Now don't ask about royalty or we'll have to get into why in the past humanity was drawn to servility and being led. There's that fear thing again which makes people do things contrary to their better sense.

Great-grandson: Were you a pleb or patrician when it mattered?

Grandpa: Neither, I was just good-looking.

Great-grandson: Ha ha. And crazy!! What did you say about rapid change?

Grandpa: Ha ha. So true.

POSTSCRIPT

Annual Meeting of the Mighty Blue Historical Progress Committee: June 2202

Agenda: Historical Landscape Review – Yellow Alert.
Info System Directive: Address Herstel Fidia (Chief Adjuster: Historical Landscape)

Herstel, there appears to be an unusual series of events in our past. Slightly off course, not on our natural path. If it continues, it will affect our present.

We have to ensure the course in the past is on the right trajectory.

You cannot change the past, but you can instruct humanity to tread the right path. You have limited informational tools to assist in the process.

You are to go there immediately and prepare them to correct their trajectory. Humanity does tend to stray at times. This is no different than the early twentieth century global conflict.

As you did then, we are confident you will set humanity of its proper course.

Safe journey.

APPENDIX

This section mirrors the Blue Notes which appear on Mighty Blue to assist visitors in reviewing the statistical and factual information pertaining to the subject matters referred to in the Doctrine. Herstel's call to action notes for each subject appear in italics – as a matter of record.

GLOBAL DEBT (2022): 307 T$

Corporate 161.7T$
Personal 57.6T$
Government 85.7T$
- USA 30.11T$
- China 14.00T$
- Japan 10.17T$

COUNTRIES SPENDING MORE THAN
THEY MAKE (expenses as %of GDP)

- Japan 239.1
- Greece 197
- Singapore 165.1

- Italy 134.8
- USA 116.1
- Portugal 109.3
- France 107.7
- Spain 106.2
- Bulgaria 106.0

GLOBAL WEALTH DOUBLED 1995-2018
Low income countries increased by 1%
Low middle income countries by 7%
Upper middle-income countries by 32%
High income(non-OECD) 3%
High income OECD 58%

Who owns the worlds wealth? (remove restrictions and provide tools for poor to prosper)

> Countries in the Global North(21% of global population) own 69% of global wealth. Top 1% own 43% of global financial assets.
> Total wealth of world.
> Net private wealth $454.4T (2022)
> Assets $1,540T (2020)

What percentage of the world is poor?

> Estimates for 2022 suggest that 46 million more people were living on less than the $3.65 poverty line than in 2019. As of 2022, 23% of the global population (1.8 billion people) were living on less than this threshold
> Currently, 1 billion people worldwide live on less than one dollar a day, the threshold defined by the international community as constituting extreme poverty

How much of the world is underdeveloped?

> 1.2 billion people in 111 developing countries live in multi-dimensional poverty, accounting for 19% of the world's population. 593 million children are experiencing multi-dimensional poverty. Over 37 million people were living in poverty in the U.S. in 2021. Apr 4, 2023

Total debt of world.

> The global debt reached $305T in 2022, including debt by both public and private debtors.

Who will rule the world in 2100?

> The US will still be the premier power, Russia and China will still be catching up, Europe will still be an economic powerhouse (relative to others), Africa will still suck, South America will still be ignored. India might finally come into its own and perhaps come to look a lot like China did 10 years ago. Apr 12, 2023

What is the average income of the world?

> As the world's economy has continued to grow over the past decades, so have wages and salaries, with the global net national income per capita reaching 8,700 U.S. dollars in 2020. Dec 18, 2023
> Of the seven largest developed economies, in 2022, the United States had the highest average wage by a significant margin at slightly over 77,000 U.S. dollars per year. Canada had the second highest annual average wages at around 59,050 U.S. dollars per year, and Germany followed behind with around 58,940 U.S. dollars per year. Meanwhile, Japan

had the lowest average wages out of the seven largest developed economies at around 41,509 U.S. dollars per year.

As of 2022, Zimbabwe had the lowest average monthly salary of employees in the world ($5.51) in terms of purchasing power parities (PPP), which takes the average cost of living in a country into account. Rwanda had the second lowest average wages ($93.35), with Gambia in third ($253). Of the 20 countries with the lowest average salaries in the world, 18 were located in Africa

AID

In the last sixty years, total aid has grown more than four-fold, from US$38 billion in 1960 to US$ 210.7 billion in 2022.
In the last sixty years, total aid has grown more than four-fold, from US$38

How much is given to charity globally?

The global philanthropy market is estimated to be £182 billion. People gave
£11.3 billion to charity in the UK in 2020, up from £10.6 billion in 2019.

How big is the global fundraising market?

Fundraising Market size was valued at USD 625.89 Billion in 2022 and is projected to reach USD 845.15 Billion by 2030, growing at a CAGR of 3.83% from 2024 to 2030.

How much money actually goes to charity?

How much of your donations actually go to charity? Some charities allocate 60% of donations to their cause, preserving a large portion of funds to pay staff high salaries, while others allocate 95% of their goods and funds to people in need. Jan 11, 2024

Which country gives most charity in the world?

Around the world, 4.2 billion people helped someone they didn't know, volunteered time or donated money to a good cause according to the Charities Aid Foundation's World Giving Index 2023. For the sixth year in a row, the world's most generous country is Indonesia.

What country gives the least to charity?

China has the lowest Index score over the 10 years at 16% and in fact is the only country that appears in the bottom 10 for all three measures we ask about; helping a stranger, donating money and volunteering time.

What are the disadvantages of foreign aid to developing countries?

It can be used to manipulate or control the recipient country's politics, limit its autonomy, and weaken its sovereignty. Additionally, foreign aid can create a dependence on the donor country, which can lead to long-term economic and social problems for the recipient nation.

What country spends the least on food?

The US spends the least at 6.4%, Singapore spends the second lowest amount at 6.7%. Canada spends 9.1% on food, while Australia spends 9.8%. Nigeria spends over half of household income on food, and there are nine other countries that spend over 40% on food. Dec 7, 2016

According to the U.S. News and World Report, these are the top 5 countries that receive the highest amount of foreign aid as of 2021:

- Israel ($3.3B)
- Jordan ($1.6B)
- Afghanistan ($1.4B)
- Ethiopia ($1.39B)
- Egypt ($1.29B)
- Oct 28, 2023

How many people work in the humanitarian sector?

> More than 630,000 humanitarian staff were estimated to be working in countries with humanitarian crises in 2020. Over 90% of these staff were nationals of the countries they were working in. Source: Humanitarian Outcomes, Global Database of Humanitarian Organizations.

ARMS (drastically reduce civilian and military ownership)

What is the total global military expenditure?

> The value of military spending globally has grown steadily in the past years and reached 2.24 trillion U.S. dollars in 2022.Nov 30, 2023

Global arms ownership.

> The world's armed forces control about 133 million (approximately 18 percent) of the global total of small arms, of which over 43 percent belong to two countries: Russia (30.3 million) and China (27.5 million). Law enforcement agencies control about 23 million (about 2 percent) of the global total of small arms.

USA gun ownership.

> There are more guns in the US than people. There are
> about 393 million privately owned firearms in the US,
> according to an estimate by the Switzerland-based Small
> Arms Survey – or in other words, 120 guns for every 100
> Americans. Jun 2, 2022

Who are the top 10 arms importers in the world?

> The top 10 largest arms importers in the world include
> India, Saudi Arabia, Qatar, Australia, China, Egypt,
> South Korea, Pakistan, Japan and the US. The global arms
> trade is a significant aspect of geopolitics and international
> relations. Jun 5, 2023

RELIGION (abolish organised religion)

Ranking - Name - Net worth

1 The Church of Jesus Christ of Latter-day Saints $100 billion
2 Catholic Church in Vatican City $30 billion
3 Church of England About $28.9 billion
4 Catholic Church in Germany $26 billion
5 Catholic Church in Australia $20.5 billion
6 Seventh Day Adventist At least $15.6 billion
7 Trinity Church $6 billion
8 Opus Dei $2.8 billion
9 The Episcopal Church $2.4 billion
10 Church of Scientology $2 billion
11 Catholic Church in the Philippines $2 billion
12 Protestant Church of Germany $1 billion
13 Cathedral Notrc-Dame de Paris $1 billion
14 Kenneth Copeland Ministries About $800 million

TOTAL INHERITED WEALTH (limit to what can be passed on)

> In the next 20 to 30 years, wealth worth around $5.2 tril-
> lion is expected to be passed from one generation to an-
> other. "The great wealth transfer is gaining significant mo-
> mentum," Benjamin Cavalli, head of UBS global wealth
> management strategic clients, told reporters in a briefing
> on Wednesday.Nov 30, 2023
> Of the 137 people in the global study who achieved bil-
> lionaire status in the 12-month study period, 53 of them
> inherited $150.8 billion collectively, more than the $140.7
> billion that was earned by the 84 new self-made billion-
> aires in the same time period, the UBS study says.

MOBILE PHONES OWNERSHIP GLOBALLY (get a phone to everyone)

Number of Smartphone Users Worldwide (Billions)
Year - Number of smartphones (in billions) - Number of smartphone users (in billions)

Year	Smartphones	Users
2029	8.06	6.38
2028	7.95	6.22
2027	7.77	6.01
2026	7.58	5.65
2025	7.43	5.28
2024	7.21	4.88
2023	6.97	4.25
2022	6.62	3.62
2021	6.34	3.10
2020	5.92	2.67
2019	5.59	2.27
2018	5.05	1.94
2017	4.45	1.66
2016	3.70	1.43

2015   3.00   1.22
2014   2.33   1.01

*Forecast figures by Ericsson (Source: https://www.bankmycell.com/blog/how-many-phones-are-in-the-world)

What percentage of the world has a bank account? (access to digital accounts through Mighty Blue)

Adults with an account (%), 2011–2021

> Worldwide account ownership has reached 76 percent of the global population—and 71 percent of people in developing countries. The gender gap in account ownership across developing economies has fallen to 6 percentage points from 9 percentage points, where it hovered for many years.

How many people don t have access to good health? (distribute basic medicine to all)

> World Bank and WHO: Half the world lacks access to essential health services, 100 million still pushed into extreme poverty because of health expenses. At least half of the world's population cannot obtain essential health services, according to a new report from the World Bank and WHO. Dec 13, 2017

What percent of people lack clean water?

> Almost three-quarters of the world's population uses to a safely managed water source. One in four people does not use a safe drinking water source. In the next chart, we see the breakdown of drinking water use globally and across regions and income groups.

VALUE OF REPARATIONS (begin payments immediately- hf)

> In 1999, the African World Reparations and Repatriation Truth Commission called for the West to pay $777 (~$1.29 quadrillion in 2022) trillion to Africa within five years.

How much do black reparations cost?

> SAN FRANCISCO (AP) — It could cost California more than $800 billion to compensate Black residents for generations of over-policing, disproportionate incarceration and housing discrimination, economists have told a state panel considering reparations. Mar 29, 2023

Who does the United States pay reparations to?

> Author A. Kirsten Mullen pointed out that the United States government has paid reparations to Japanese families who were interned during World War II, families who lost loved ones during the Sept. 11 attacks, and to Americans held hostage in Iran. May 17, 2022

How much would reparations cost the US?

> He estimates a fair reparation value anywhere between $1.4 to $4.7 trillion, or roughly $142,000 (equivalent to $175,000 in 2022) for every black American living today. Other estimates range from $5.7 to $14.2 and $17.1 trillion.

Does Germany owe the US money for ww2?

> After World War II, according to the Potsdam conference held between July 17 and August 2, 1945, Germany was

to pay the Allies US$23 billion mainly in machinery and manufacturing plants. Dismantling in the West stopped in 1950. Reparations to the Soviet Union stopped in 1953 (only paid by the GDR).

Does Germany still pay money to Israel?

German reparation payments total some 82 billion euro (2022). Around 1.44 billion euro is paid from the federal budget each year for pension and care costs of victims of Nazi persecution, many of whom live in Israel (2022 figures). Jan 4, 2024

Why did Haiti agree to pay reparations to France after the Haitian Revolution?

You read that correctly. It was the former slaves of Haiti, not the French slaveholders, who were forced to pay reparations. Haitians compensated their oppressors and their oppressors' descendants for the privilege of being free. It took Haiti more than a century to pay the reparation debts off. Oct 5, 2021

How much did France steal from Haiti?

In 1825, Haiti Paid France $21 Billion To Preserve Its Independence -- Time for France To Pay It Back. Dec 6, 2017

INDIGENOUS

How many indigenous people were killed in the colonization of America?

According to geographers from University College London, the colonization of the Americas by Europeans killed so many people, approximately 55 million or 90% of the local populations, it resulted in climate change and global cooling.

The U.S. government has never given any direct compensation, financial or otherwise, for slavery. In fact, the United States only officially apologized for slavery in 2009. While the government has made few moves towards reparations for slavery, it has compensated other groups for the historical injustices they faced. There are many examples of this,—one (reparations for Japanese Americans) that is generally thought to be well-executed, and another (reparations for Native Americans) largely regarded as unsuccessful.

What percentage of land in Canada is owned by Indigenous?

Canada is a vast country (9.985 million sq km) but just 0.2 percent of its total landmass is reserve land. That 0.2 percent of Canada's landmass is home to 339,595 Indigenous people (2016 Census), or 0.2% of the landmass houses 20% of the Indigenous population. Nov 27, 2018

How much has Canada paid in reparations?

The class action lawsuit by 325 Indigenous groups ended with the settlement of 2.8 billion Canadian dollars ($2.1bn United States) which will be placed in a trust fund independent of the government. Jan 22, 2023

How much has Canada paid to Indigenous?

The federal government has been ordered to pay $23 billion to First Nations kids and families. The compensation is for years of underfunding on-reserve social assistance.

This includes funding for housing, education, health care and other forms of help. Nov 6, 2023

Australia: What did the Aboriginal population decrease by in the first 150 years the British were in Australia?

> After invasion on 26 January 1788, Indigenous people were almost decimated by massacres and widespread poisoning, imprisonment, the forced removal of children and programs of assimilation and racial "dilution". By federation in 1901, the Aboriginal and Torres Strait Islander population had diminished to about 117,000. May 18, 2017

New Zealand: How many Māori died during colonization?

> There is a common belief that musket warfare between 1810 and 1840 caused heavy mortality among Māori. However, war deaths were not great in number compared with the deaths from other causes. From 1810 to 1840 there were around 120,000 deaths from illness and other 'normal' causes, an average of 4,000 a year. May 5, 2011 New Zealand's Māori fought for reparations — and won. The country has leaped far ahead of others on redressing the wrongs of its past. While the program isn't perfect, it has lessons to teach the US.

Indigenous – British empire – 10 billion pounds

> The origins of the C of E's £10bn endowment fund were partly traced to Queen Anne's Bounty, a financial scheme established in 1704 based on transatlantic chattel slavery.

Fast facts: Global poverty

- 719 million people — 9.2% of the world's population — are living on less than $2.15 a day.
- Children and youth account for two-thirds of the world's poor, and women represent a majority in most regions.
- Extreme poverty is largely concentrated in sub-Saharan Africa.
- 24% of the world's population, which equates to 1.9 billion people, live in fragile contexts, characterized by impoverished conditions and dire circumstances.
- By 2030, more than half of the world's poor will live in fragile contexts.
- About 63% of people older than 15 who live in extreme poverty have no schooling or only some basic education.
- 1.2 billion people in 111 developing countries live in multi-dimensional poverty, accounting for 19% of the world's population.
- 593 million children are experiencing multidimensional poverty.
- Over 37 million people were living in poverty in the U.S. in 2021. Children account for 11.1 million of those.
- Earth's population is approximately 7.8 billion people

However, if you count the world's 7.8 billion people as 100% human, these percentages become clearer.

From 100% of people:

- 11% are in Europe
- 5% is in North America
- 9% - in South America
- 15% - in Africa

- 60% are in Asia
- 49% live in villages.
- 51% - In cities
- 62% in their own language
- 77% have housing
- 23% have nowhere to live.
- 21% of people eat in excess
- 63% can eat as much as they want
- 15% of the people are malnourished
- 87% of people have clean drinking water
- 13% either do not have clean drinking water or have access to a contaminated water source.
- 30% have internet access
- 70% do not have internet access
- 7% received higher studies
- 93% of people never went to college or university.
- 17% of people are illiterate.

How can we break the cycle of extreme poverty? (economic disadvantage is the crippling factor)

> To break the cycle of poverty, we need to tackle its root causes, including economic inequality; lack of access to education, healthcare, and infrastructure; and discrimination. Identifying what's causing poverty in a particular community can equip people to determine what needs to change. Because it looks different in various places and is caused by different factors, the work to eradicate extreme poverty varies on the context.
>
> To end extreme poverty by 2030, the U.N. estimates that it would take about $350 billion per year in funding beyond work already happening.(equate with global wealth, corporate wealth, global income and inherited wealth)

What is the international poverty line?

> The international poverty line, recently updated to $2.15 a day to show more accurately the cost of basic items and to adjust for inflation, is the universal standard for measuring global poverty. This line helps measure the number of people living in extreme poverty and helps compare poverty levels between countries.
>
> As the cost of living increases, poverty lines increase too. Since 1990, the international poverty line has risen from $1 a day, to $1.25 daily, and in 2015 to $1.90. The figure rose from $1.90 to $2.15 in September 2022. This means that $2.15 is necessary to buy what $1 could in 1990.
>
> In addition to the lowest-income poverty line at $2.15, the World Bank also reports poverty rates using two new international poverty lines: a lower middle-income line at $3.65 a day and an upper middle-income line at $6.85 a day.

Total household wealth by country

Top 10 countries by total wealth, 2022

> United States (30.8%)
> China (18.6%)
> Japan (5.0%)
> Germany (3.8%)
> United Kingdom (3.5%)
> France (3.5%)
> India (5.0%)
> Canada (2.5%)
> Italy (2.4%)
> South Korea (2.2%)
> Rest of the World (24.4%)

HERSTEL AND FRIENDS IN HIGH PLACES (those who really govern and are responsible for the direction of humanity and its resources. the concentration of power was orchestrated by friends in high places. The dissolution of power will utilise a similar working model)

The concentration of monetary power governed by a small number of powerful organisations who were largely unelected and formed in an undemocratic process makes it near impossible for the disadvantaged to stand on their own two feet. Herstel actions dissipates this power and re-distributes the wealth. Those in control presently are unable to prevent the changes. They can continue their pursuit of power and monetary gain, but they will not be help by the masses who with the help and guidance of Mighty Blue are awakening to and pursuing a life of meaningful activities and goals unconnected to material gains.

ORGANISATIONS and INDIVIDUALS EMBEDDED WITH GLOBAL ECONOMIC AND POLITAL POWER.

UNITED NATIONS (STAFF 125,436 – 2022)

BANK OF INTERNATIONAL SETTLEMENTS (STAFF 1300)

Our mission is to support central banks' pursuit of monetary and financial stability through international cooperation, and to act as a bank for central banks.

Established in 1930, the BIS is owned by 63 central banks, representing countries from around the world that together account for about 95% of world GDP. (there is a noticeable lack of African, Arab, and LDC memberships- hf)

KLAUS SCHWAB

Klaus Martin Schwab (German: born 30 March 1938) is a German mechanical engineer, economist, and founder of the World Economic Forum (WEF). He has acted as the WEF›s chairman since founding the organisation in 1971.

In 1971, Schwab founded the European Management Forum, which was renamed as the World Economic Forum in 1987. In 1971, he also published Moderne Unternehmensführung im Maschinenbau.

In 2003 Schwab appointed José María Figueres CEO of the WEF, as his successor. In October 2004, Figueres resigned over his undeclared receipt of more than US$900,000 in consultancy fees from the French telecommunications firm Alcatel while he was working at the Forum. In 2006, Transparency International highlighted this incident in their Global Corruption Report.

Schwab founded the Global Shapers Community in 2011 within the WEF to work with young people in "shaping local, regional and global agendas."

In 2015, the WEF was formally recognised by the Swiss Government as an "international body".

AS AUTHOR:

Schwab has authored or co-authored several books. Some consider him to be "an evangelist" for "stakeholder capitalism". The Fourth Industrial Revolution, the subject of a 2016 book he wrote, is an idea he is credited with popularising. In January 2017 Steven Poole in The Guardian criticized Schwab›s Fourth Industrial Revolution book, pointing out that "the internet of things" would probably be hackable. He also criticized Schwab for showing that future technologies may be used for good or evil, but not taking a position on the issues, instead offering only vague policy recommendations. The Financial Times' innovation editor found "the clunking lifelessness of the prose" led him to "suspect this book really was written by humans—ones who inhabit a strange twilight world of stakeholders, externalities, inflection points and ‹developtory sandboxes'."

The political scientist Klaus-Gerd Giesen has argued that the dominant ideology of the Fourth Industrial Revolution is transhumanism.

CRITICISM

Salary level and lack of financial transparency
While Schwab declared that excessively high management salaries were

"no longer socially acceptable", his own annual salary of about one million Swiss francs (a little more than $1 million USD) has been repeatedly questioned by the media. The Swiss radio and television corporation SRF mentioned this salary level in the context of ongoing public contributions to the WEF and the fact that the Forum does not pay any federal taxes. Moreover, the former Frankfurter Allgemeine Zeitung journalist Jürgen Dunsch made the criticism that the WEF's financial reports were not very transparent since neither income nor expenditures were broken down. Schwab has also drawn ire for mixing the finances of the not-for-profit WEF and other for-profit business ventures. For example, the WEF awarded a multimillion dollar contract to US Web in 1998. Yet shortly after the deal went through, Schwab took a board seat at the same company, reaping valuable stock options.

WORLD ECONOMIC FORUM (STAFF 800)

The World Economic Forum (WEF) is an international non-governmental organization based in Cologny, Canton of Geneva, Switzerland. It was founded on 24 January 1971 by German engineer Klaus Schwab.

The foundation's stated mission is "improving the state of the world by engaging business, political, academic, and other leaders of society to shape global, regional, and industry agendas". The Forum states that the world is best managed by a self-selected coalition of multinational corporations, governments and civil society organizations (CSOs), which it expresses through initiatives like the "Great Reset"[3] and the "Global Redesign".

The foundation is mostly funded by its 1,000 member multi-national companies.

The WEF is mostly known for its annual meeting at the end of January in Davos, a mountain resort in the eastern Alps region of Switzerland. The meeting brings together some 3,000 paying members and selected participants – among whom are investors, business leaders, political leaders, economists, celebrities and journalists – for up to five days to discuss global issues across 500 sessions.

Aside from Davos, the organization convenes regional conferences. It produces a series of reports, engages its members in sector-specific initiatives[6] and provides a platform for leaders from selected stakeholder groups to collaborate on projects and initiatives.[7]

The World Economic Forum and its annual meeting in Davos have received criticism over the years, including allegations[of the organization's corporate capture of global and democratic institutions, institutional whitewashing initiatives, the public cost of security, the organization's tax-exempt status, unclear decision processes and membership criteria, a lack of financial transparency, and the environmental footprint of its annual meetings

BOARD OF TRUSTEES

The WEF is chaired by founder and executive chairman Professor Klaus Schwab and is guided by a board of trustees that is made up of leaders from business, politics, academia and civil society. In 2010 the board was composed of: Josef Ackermann, Peter Brabeck-Letmathe, Kofi Annan, Victor L. L. Chu, Tony Blair, Michael Dell, Niall FitzGerald, Susan Hockfield, Orit Gadiesh, Christine Lagarde, Carlos Ghosn, Maurice Lévy, Rajat Gupta, Indra Nooyi, Peter D. Sutherland, Ivan Pictet   Heizō Takenaka, Ernesto Zedillo, Joseph P. Schoendorf and Queen Rania of Jordan.[9] Members of the board of trustees (past or present) include: Mukesh Ambani, Marc Benioff, Peter Brabeck-Letmathe, Mark Carney, Laurence Fink, Chrystia Freeland, Orit Gadiesh, Fabiola Gianotti, Al Gore, Herman Gref, José Ángel Gurría, André Hoffmann, Ursula von der Leyen, Jack Ma, Yo-Yo Ma, Peter Maurer, Luis Alberto Moreno, Muriel Pénicaud, Queen Rania of Jordan, Leo Rafael Reif, David Rubenstein, Mark Schneider, Klaus Schwab, Tharman Shanmugaratnam, Jim Hagemann Snabe , Feike Sijbesma, Heizō Takenaka, Zhu Min.

MEMBERSHIP (1000)

The foundation is funded by its 1,000 member companies, typically global enterprises with more than five billion dollars in turnover (varying by industry and region). These enterprises rank among the top companies within their industry and/or country and play a leading role in shaping the future of their industry and/or region. Membership is stratified by the level of engagement with forum activities, with the level of membership fees increasing as participation in meetings, projects, and initiatives rises. In 2011, an annual membership cost $52,000 for an individual member, $263,000 for "Industry Partner" and $527,000 for "Strategic Partner". An admission fee costs $19,000 per person. In 2014, WEF raised annual fees by 20 percent, bringing the cost for "Strategic Partner" from CHF 500,000 ($523,000) to CHF 600,000 ($628,000).

WORLD TRADE ORGANISATION (STAFF 620)

The World Trade Organization (WTO) is an intergovernmental organization headquartered in Geneva, Switzerland[6] that regulates and facilitates international trade.[7] Governments use the organization to establish, revise, and enforce the rules that govern international trade in cooperation with the United Nations System.[7][8] The WTO is the world's largest international economic organization, with 164 member states representing over 98% of global trade and global GDP

ACCESSION AND MEMBERSHIP

The process of becoming a WTO member is unique to each applicant country, and the terms of accession are dependent upon the country's stage of economic development and the current trade regime.[99] The process takes about five years, on average, but it can last longer if the country is less than fully committed to the process or if political issues interfere. The shortest accession negotiation was that of the Kyrgyz Republic, while the longest was that of Russia, which, having first applied to join GATT in 1993, was approved for membership in December 2011 and became a WTO member on 22 August 2012.[100] Kazakhstan also had a long accession negotiation process. The Working Party on the Accession of Kazakhstan was established in 1996 and was approved for membership in 2015.[101] The second longest was that of Vanuatu, whose Working Party on the Accession of Vanuatu was established on 11 July 1995. After a final meeting of the Working Party in October 2001, Vanuatu requested more time to consider its accession terms. In 2008, it indicated its interest to resume and conclude its WTO accession. The Working Party on the Accession of Vanuatu was reconvened informally on 4 April 2011 to discuss Vanuatu's future WTO membership.

The re-convened Working Party completed its mandate on 2 May 2011. The General Council formally approved the Accession Package of Vanuatu on 26 October 2011. On 24 August 2012, the WTO welcomed Vanuatu as its 157th member. An offer of accession is only given once consensus is reached among interested parties.

A 2017 study argues that "political ties rather than issue-area functional gains determine who joins" and shows "how geopolitical alignment shapes the demand and supply sides of membership". The "findings challenge the view that states first liberalize trade to join the GATT/WTO. Instead, democracy and foreign policy similarity encourage states to join."

As of 2007, WTO member states represented 96.4% of global trade and 96.7% of global GDP. Iran, followed by Algeria, are the economies with the largest GDP and trade outside the WTO, using 2005 data. With the exception of the Holy See, observers must start accession negotiations within five years of becoming observers. A number of international intergovernmental organizations have also been granted observer status to WTO bodies. Ten UN members have no affiliation with the WTO.

BUDGET

The WTO derives most of the income for its annual budget from contributions by its Members. These are established according to a formula based on their share of international trade.

2019 TOP 10 MEMBERS' CONTRIBUTIONS TO THE CONSOLIDATED BUDGET OF THE WTO[133]

Rank	Country	CHF	Percentage
1	United States	22,660,405	11.59%
2	China	19,737,680	10.10%
3	Germany	13,882,455	7.10%

4	Japan	7,896,245	4.04%
5	United Kingdom	7,446,595	3.81%
6	France	7,440,730	3.81%
7	South Korea	5,777,025	2.96%
8	Netherlands	5,745,745	2.94%
9	Hong Kong	5,427,080	2.78%
10	Italy	5,096,685	2.61%
Others		94,389,355	48.28%
TOTAL		195,500,000	100%

CRITICISM

Although tariffs and other trade barriers have been significantly reduced thanks to GATT and WTO, the promise that free trade will accelerate economic growth, reduce poverty, and increase people's incomes has been questioned by many critics.[25]

Economist Ha-Joon Chang argues that there is a "paradox" in neo-liberal beliefs regarding free trade because the economic growth of developing countries was higher in the 1960–1980 period compared to the 1980–2000 period even though its trade policies are now far more liberal than before. Also, there are results of research that show that new countries actively reduce trade barriers only after becoming significantly rich. From the results of the study, WTO critics argue that trade liberalization does not guarantee economic growth and certainly not poverty alleviation.[25] He also cites the example of El Salvador; in the early 1990s, El Salvador removed all quantitative barriers to imports and also cut tariffs. However, the country's economic growth remained weak. On the other hand, Vietnam, which only began reforming its economy in the late 1980s, saw a great deal of success by deciding to follow China's economic model and liberalizing slowly along with implementing safeguards for domestic commerce. Vietnam has largely succeeded in accelerating economic growth and reducing poverty without immediately removing substantial trade barriers.

Critics also put forward the view that the benefits derived from WTO facilitated free trade are not shared equally.[26] This criticism is usually supported by historical accounts of the outcomes of negotiations and/or data showing that the gap between the rich and the poor continues to widen, especially in China and India, where economic inequality was growing at the time even though economic growth is very high.[25] In addition, WTO approaches aiming to reduce trade barriers can harm developing countries. Trade liberalization that is too early without any prominent domestic barriers is feared to trap the developing economies in the primary sector, which often does not require skilled labor. And when these developing countries decide to advance their economy utilizing industrialization, the premature domestic industry cannot immediately skyrocket as expected, making it difficult to compete with other countries whose industries are more advanced.

IMPACT

Studies show that the WTO boosted trade. Research shows that in the absence of the WTO, the average country would face an increase in tariffs on their exports by 32 percentage points. The dispute settlement mechanism in the WTO is one way in which trade is increased.

According to a 2017 study in the Journal of International Economic Law, "nearly all recent preferential trade agreements (PTAs) reference the WTO explicitly, often dozens of times across multiple chapters. Likewise, in many of these same PTAs we find that substantial portions of treaty language—sometime the majority of a chapter—is copied verbatim from a WTO agreement... the presence of the WTO in PTAs has increased over time."

INTERNATIONAL MONETARY FUND (STAFF 3000)

The International Monetary Fund (IMF) is a major financial agency of the United Nations, and an international financial institution funded by 190 member countries, with headquarters in Washington, D.C. It is regarded as the global lender of last resort to national governments, and a leading supporter of exchange-rate stability. Its stated mission is "working to foster global monetary cooperation, secure financial stability, facilitate international trade, promote high employment and sustainable economic growth, and reduce poverty around the world." Established on December 27, 1945¹at the Bretton Woods Conference, primarily according to the ideas of Harry Dexter White and John Maynard Keynes, it started with 29 member countries and the goal of reconstructing the international monetary system after World War II. It now plays a central role in the management of balance of payments difficulties and international financial crises. Through a quota system, countries contribute funds to a pool from which countries can borrow if they experience balance of payments problems. As of 2016, the fund had SDR 477 billion (about US$667 billion).

The IMF works to stabilize and foster the economies of its member countries by its use of the fund, as well as other activities such as gathering and analyzing economic statistics and surveillance of its members' economies. IMF funds come from two major sources: quotas and loans. Quotas, which are pooled funds from member nations, generate most IMF funds. The size of members' quotas increase according to their economic and financial importance in the world. The quotas are increased periodically as a means of boosting the IMF's resources in the form of special drawing rights.

The current managing director (MD) and chairwoman of the IMF is Bulgarian economist Kristalina Georgieva, who has held the post since October 1, 2019. Indian-American economist Gita Gopinath, previously the chief economist, was appointed as first deputy managing director, effective January 21, 2022.[16] Pierre-Olivier Gourinchas was appointed chief economist on January 24, 2022.

FUNCTIONS
According to the IMF itself, it works to foster global growth and economic stability by providing policy advice and financing the members by working with developing countries to help them achieve macroeconomic stability and reduce poverty. The rationale for this is that private international capital markets function imperfectly and many countries have limited access to financial markets. Such market imperfections, together with balance-of-payments financing, provide the justification for official financing, without which many

countries could only correct large external payment imbalances through measures with adverse economic consequences. The IMF provides alternate sources of financing such as the Poverty Reduction and Growth Facility.

Upon the founding of the IMF, its three primary functions were:

- to oversee the fixed exchange rate arrangements between countries, thus helping national governments manage their exchange rates and allowing these governments to prioritize economic growth, and
- to provide short-term capital to aid the balance of payments and prevent the spread of international economic crises.
- to help mend the pieces of the international economy after the Great Depression and World War II[as well as to provide capital investments for economic growth and projects such as infrastructure.

The IMF's role was fundamentally altered by the floating exchange rates after 1971. It shifted to examining the economic policies of countries with IMF loan agreements to determine whether a shortage of capital was due to economic fluctuations or economic policy. The IMF also researched what types of government policy would ensure economic recovery. A particular concern of the IMF was to prevent financial crises, such as those in Mexico in 1982, Brazil in 1987, East Asia in 1997–98, and Russia in 1998, from spreading and threatening the entire global financial and currency system. The challenge was to promote and implement a policy that reduced the frequency of crises among emerging market countries, especially the middle-income countries which are vulnerable to massive capital outflows. Rather than maintaining a position of oversight of only exchange rates, their function became one of surveillance of the overall macroeconomic performance of member countries. Their role became a lot more active because the IMF now manages economic policy rather than just exchange rates.

In addition, the IMF negotiates conditions on lending and loans under their policy of conditionality, which was established in the 1950s.

Low-income countries can borrow on concessional terms, which means there is a period of time with no interest rates, through the Extended Credit Facility (ECF), the Standby Credit Facility (SCF) and the Rapid Credit Facility (RCF). Non-concessional loans, which include interest rates, are provided mainly through the Stand-By Arrangements (SBA), the Flexible Credit Line (FCL), the Precautionary and Liquidity Line (PLL), and the Extended Fund Facility. The IMF provides emergency assistance via the Rapid Financing Instrument (RFI) to members facing urgent balance-of-payments needs.

SURVEILLANCE OF THE GLOBAL ECONOMY

The IMF is mandated to oversee the international monetary and financial system and monitor the economic and financial policies of its member countries. This activity is known as surveillance and facilitates international co-operation. Since the demise of the Bretton Woods system of fixed exchange rates in the early 1970s, surveillance has evolved largely by way of changes in procedures rather than through the adoption of new obligations. The responsibilities changed from those of guardians to those of overseers of members› policies.

The Fund typically analyses the appropriateness of each member country's economic and financial policies for achieving orderly economic growth, and assesses the consequences of these policies for other countries and for the global economy. For instance, The IMF played a significant role in individual countries, such as Armenia and Belarus, in providing financial support to achieve stabilization financing from 2009 to 2019. The maximum sustainable debt level of a polity, which is watched closely by the IMF, was defined in 2011 by IMF economists to be 120%. Indeed, it was at this number that the Greek economy melted down in 2010.

PARTICIPANTS:

IMF member using SDDS
IMF member using GDDS
IMF member, not using any of the Systems
non-IMF entity using SDDS

non-IMF entity using GDDS
no interaction with the IMF

In 1995, the International Monetary Fund began to work on data dissemination standards with the view of guiding IMF member countries to disseminate their economic and financial data to the public. The International Monetary and Financial Committee (IMFC) endorsed the guidelines for the dissemination standards and they were split into two tiers: The General Data Dissemination System (GDDS) and the Special Data Dissemination Standard (SDDS).

The executive board approved the SDDS and GDDS in 1996 and 1997, respectively, and subsequent amendments were published in a revised Guide to the General Data Dissemination System. The system is aimed primarily at statisticians and aims to improve many aspects of statistical systems in a country. It is also part of the World Bank Millennium Development Goals (MDG) and Poverty Reduction Strategic Papers (PRSPs)

The primary objective of the GDDS is to encourage member countries to build a framework to improve data quality and statistical capacity building to evaluate statistical needs, set priorities in improving timeliness, transparency, reliability, and accessibility of financial and economic data. Some countries initially used the GDDS, but later upgraded to SDDS.

Some entities that are not IMF members also contribute statistical data to the systems:

- Palestinian Authority – GDDS
- Hong Kong – SDDS
- Macau – GDDS
- Institutions of the European Union:
    - The European Central Bank for the Eurozone – SDDS
    - Eurostat for the whole EU – SDDS, thus providing data from Cyprus (not using any System on its own) and Malta (using only GDDS on its own)

A 2021 study found that the IMF's surveillance activities have "a substantial impact on sovereign debt with much greater impacts in emerging than high-income economies".

CONDITIONALITY OF LOANS

IMF conditionality is a set of policies or conditions that the IMF requires in exchange for financial resources.[21] The IMF does require collateral from countries for loans but also requires the government seeking assistance to correct its macroeconomic imbalances in the form of policy reform.[35] If the conditions are not met, the funds are withheld.[21][36] The concept of conditionality was introduced in a 1952 executive board decision and later incorporated into the Articles of Agreement.

Conditionality is associated with economic theory as well as an enforcement mechanism for repayment. Stemming primarily from the work of Jacques Polak, the theoretical underpinning of conditionality was the "monetary approach to the balance of payments".[22]

Some of the conditions for structural adjustment can include:

- Cutting expenditures or raising revenues, also known as austerity.
- Focusing economic output on direct export and resource extraction,
- Devaluation of currencies,
- Trade liberalisation, or lifting import and export restrictions,
- Increasing the stability of investment (by supplementing foreign direct investment with the opening of facilities for the domestic market),
- Balancing budgets and not overspending,
- Removing price controls and state subsidies,
- Privatization, or divestiture of all or part of state-owned enterprises,
- Enhancing the rights of foreign investors vis-a-vis national laws,

- Improving governance and fighting corruption,

These conditions are known as the Washington Consensus.

BENEFITS

These loan conditions ensure that the borrowing country will be able to repay the IMF and that the country will not attempt to solve their balance-of-payment problems in a way that would negatively impact the international economy. The incentive problem of moral hazard—when economic agents maximise their own utility to the detriment of others because they do not bear the full consequences of their actions—is mitigated through conditions rather than providing collateral; countries in need of IMF loans do not generally possess internationally valuable collateral anyway.

Conditionality also reassures the IMF that the funds lent to them will be used for the purposes defined by the Articles of Agreement and provides safeguards that the country will be able to rectify its macroeconomic and structural imbalances. In the judgment of the IMF, the adoption by the member of certain corrective measures or policies will allow it to repay the IMF, thereby ensuring that the resources will be available to support other members.

As of 2004, borrowing countries have had a good track record for repaying credit extended under the IMF's regular lending facilities with full interest over the duration of the loan. This indicates that IMF lending does not impose a burden on creditor countries, as lending countries receive market-rate interest on most of their quota subscription, plus any of their own-currency subscriptions that are loaned out by the IMF, plus all of the reserve assets that they provide the IMF.

IMPACT

According to a 2002 study by Randall W. Stone, the academic literature on the IMF shows "no consensus on the long-term effects of IMF programs on growth".

Some research has found that IMF loans can reduce the chance of a future banking crisis, while other studies have found that they can increase the risk of political crises. IMF programs can reduce the effects of a currency crisis.

Some research has found that IMF programs are less effective in countries which possess a developed-country patron (be it by foreign aid, membership of postcolonial institutions or UN voting patterns), seemingly due to this patron allowing countries to flaunt IMF program rules as these rules are not consistently enforced. Some research has found that IMF loans reduce economic growth due to creating an economic moral hazard, reducing public investment, reducing incentives to create a robust domestic policies and reducing private investor confidence. Other research has indicated that IMF loans can have a positive impact on economic growth and that their effects are highly nuanced.

CRITICISMS

Overseas Development Institute (ODI) research undertaken in 1980 included criticisms of the IMF which support the analysis that it is a pillar of what activist Titus Alexander calls global apartheid.

Developed countries were seen to have a more dominant role and control over less developed countries (LDCs).

The Fund worked on the incorrect assumption that all payments disequilibria were caused domestically. The Group of 24 (G-24), on behalf of LDC members, and the United Nations Conference on Trade and Development (UNCTAD) complained that the IMF did not distinguish sufficiently between disequilibria with predominantly external as opposed to internal causes. This criticism was voiced in the aftermath of the 1973 oil crisis. Then LDCs found themselves with payment deficits due to adverse changes in their terms of trade, with the Fund prescribing stabilization programmes similar to those suggested for deficits caused by government over-spending. Faced with long-term, externally generated disequilibria, the G-24 argued for more time for LDCs to adjust their economies.

Some IMF policies may be anti-developmental; the report said that deflationary effects of IMF programmes quickly led to losses of output and employment in economies where incomes were low and unemployment was high. Moreover, the burden of the deflation is disproportionately borne by the poor.

The IMF's initial policies were based in theory and influenced by differing opinions and departmental rivalries. Critics suggest that its intentions to implement these policies in countries with widely varying economic circumstances were misinformed and lacked economic rationale.

ODI conclusions were that the IMF's very nature of promoting market-oriented approaches attracted unavoidable criticism. On the other hand, the IMF could serve as a scapegoat while allowing governments to blame international bankers. The ODI conceded that the IMF was insensitive to political aspirations of LDCs while its policy conditions were inflexible.

Argentina, which had been considered by the IMF to be a model country in its compliance to policy proposals by the Bretton Woods institutions, experienced a catastrophic economic crisis in 2001, which some believe to have been caused by IMF-induced budget restrictions—which undercut the government's ability to sustain national infrastructure even in crucial areas such as health, education, and security—and privatisation of strategically vital national resources.[144] Others attribute the crisis to Argentina's misdesigned fiscal federalism, which caused subnational spending to increase rapidly. The crisis added to widespread hatred of this institution in Argentina and other South American countries, with many blaming the IMF for the region's economic problems. The current—as of early 2006—trend toward moderate left-wing governments in the region and a growing concern with the development of a regional economic policy largely independent of big business pressures has been ascribed to this crisis.

In 2006, a senior ActionAid policy analyst Akanksha Marphatia stated that IMF policies in Africa undermine any possibility of meeting the Millennium Development Goals (MDGs) due to imposed restrictions that prevent spending on important sectors, such as education and health.

In an interview (2008-05-19), the former Romanian Prime Minister Călin Popescu-Tăriceanu claimed that "Since 2005, IMF is constantly making mistakes when it appreciates the country's economic performances". Former Tanzanian President Julius Nyerere, who claimed that debt-ridden African states were ceding sovereignty to the IMF and the World Bank, famously asked, "Who elected the IMF to be the ministry of finance for every country in the world?"

Former chief economist of IMF and former Reserve Bank of India (RBI) Governor Raghuram Rajan who predicted the financial crisis of 2007–08 criticized the IMF for remaining a sideline player to the developed world. He criticized the IMF for praising the monetary policies of the US, which he believed were wreaking havoc in emerging markets. He had been critical of "ultra-loose money policies" of some unnamed countries.

Countries such as Zambia have not received proper aid with long-lasting effects, leading to concern from economists. Since 2005, Zambia (as well as 29 other African countries) did receive debt write-offs, which helped with the country's medical and education funds. However, Zambia returned to a debt of over half its GDP in less than a decade. American economist William Easterly, sceptical of the IMF's methods, had initially warned that "debt relief would simply encourage more reckless borrowing by crooked governments unless it was accompanied by reforms to speed up economic growth and improve governance", according to The Economist.

CONDITIONALITY

The IMF has been criticized for being "out of touch" with local economic conditions, cultures, and environments in the countries they are requiring policy reform. The economic advice the IMF gives might not always take into consideration the difference between what spending means on paper and how it is felt by citizens. Countries charge that with excessive conditionality, they do not "own" the programmes and the links are broken between a recipient country's people, its government, and the goals being pursued by the IMF.

Jeffrey Sachs argues that the IMF's "usual prescription is ‹budgetary belt tightening to countries who are much too poor to own belts›". Sachs wrote that the IMF's role as a generalist institution specialising in macroeconomic issues needs reform. Conditionality has also been criticized because a country can pledge collateral of "acceptable assets" to obtain waivers—if one assumes that all countries are able to provide "acceptable collateral".

One view is that conditionality undermines domestic political institutions. The recipient governments are sacrificing policy autonomy in exchange for funds, which can lead to public resentment of the local leadership for accepting and enforcing the IMF conditions. Political instability can result from more leadership turnover as political leaders are replaced in electoral backlashes.[21] IMF conditions are often criticized for reducing government services, thus increasing unemployment.

Another criticism is that IMF policies are only designed to address poor governance, excessive government spending, excessive government intervention in markets, and too much state ownership. This assumes that this narrow range of issues represents the only possible problems; everything is standardised and differing contexts are ignored. A country may also be compelled to accept conditions it would not normally accept had they not been in a financial crisis in need of assistance.

On top of that, regardless of what methodologies and data sets used, it comes to the same conclusion of exacerbating income inequality. With Gini coefficient, it became clear that countries with IMF policies face increased income inequality.

It is claimed that conditionalities retard social stability and hence inhibit the stated goals of the IMF, while Structural Adjustment Programmes lead to an increase in poverty in recipient countries. The IMF sometimes advocates "austerity programmes", cutting public spending and increasing taxes even when the economy is weak, to bring budgets closer to a balance, thus reducing budget deficits. Countries are often advised to lower their corporate tax rate. In Globalization and Its Discontents, Joseph E. Stiglitz, former chief economist and senior vice-president at the World Bank, criticizes these policies. He argues that by converting to a more monetarist approach, the purpose of the fund is no longer valid, as it was designed to provide funds for countries to carry out Keynesian reflation's, and that the IMF "was not participating in a conspiracy, but it was reflecting the interests and ideology of the Western financial community."

Stiglitz concludes, "Modern high-tech warfare is designed to remove physical contact: dropping bombs from 50,000 feet ensures that one does not 'feel' what one does. Modern economic management is similar: from one's luxury hotel, one can callously impose policies about which one would think twice if one knew the people whose lives one was destroying."

The researchers Eric Toussaint and Damien Millet argue that the IMF's policies amount to a new form of colonisation that does not need a military presence:

Following the exigencies of the governments of the richest companies, the IMF, permitted countries in crisis to borrow in order to avoid default on their repayments. Caught in the debt's downward spiral, developing countries soon had no other recourse than to take on new debt in order to repay the old debt. Before providing them with new loans, at higher interest rates, future leaders asked the IMF, to intervene with the guarantee of ulterior reimbursement, asking for a signed agreement with the said countries. The IMF thus agreed to restart the flow of the 'finance pump' on condition that the concerned countries first use this money to reimburse banks and other private lenders, while restructuring their economy at the IMF's discretion: these were the famous conditionalities, detailed in the Structural Adjustment Programmes. The IMF and its ultra-liberal experts took control of the borrowing countries' economic policies. A new form of colonisation was thus instituted. It was not even necessary to establish an administrative or military presence; the debt alone maintained this new form of submission.

International politics play an important role in IMF decision making. The clout of member states is roughly proportional to its contribution to IMF finances. The United States has the greatest number of votes and therefore wields the most influence. Domestic politics often come into play, with politicians in developing countries using conditionality to gain leverage over the opposition to influence policy.

Academic Jeremy Garlick cites IMF loans to South Korea during the 1997 Asian financial crisis as widely perceived by the South Korean public as a debt-trap. Garlick writes that the public was generally bitter about submitting to the conditions imposed by the IMF, which required South Korea to radically restructure its economy and consult with the IMF before making economic decisions until the debt was repaid.

In 2016, the IMF's research department published a report titled "Neoliberalism: Oversold?" which, while praising some aspects of the "neoliberal agenda", claims that the organisation has been "overselling" fiscal austerity policies and financial deregulation, which they claim has exacerbated both financial crises and economic inequality around the world.

In 2020 and 2021, Oxfam criticized the IMF for forcing tough austerity measures on many low income countries during the COVID-19 pandemic, despite forcing cuts to healthcare spending, would hamper the recipient's response to the pandemic.

SUPPORT OF DICTATORSHIPS

The role of the Bretton Woods institutions has been controversial since the late Cold War, because of claims that the IMF policy makers supported military dictatorships friendly to American and European corporations, but also other anti-communist and Communist regimes (such as Mobutu's Zaire and Ceausescu's Romania, respectively). Critics also claim that the IMF is generally apathetic or hostile to human rights, and labour rights. The controversy has helped spark the anti-globalization movement.

An example of IMF's support for a dictatorship was its ongoing support for Mobutu's rule in Zaire, although its own envoy, Erwin Blumenthal, provided a sobering report about the entrenched corruption and embezzlement and the inability of the country to pay back any loans.

Arguments in favour of the IMF say that economic stability is a precursor to democracy; however, critics highlight various examples in which democratised countries fell after receiving IMF loans.

A 2017 study found no evidence of IMF lending programs undermining democracy in borrowing countries. To the contrary, it found "evidence for modest but definitively positive conditional differences in the democracy scores of participating and non-participating countries".

On 28 June 2021, the IMF approved a US$1 billion loan to the Ugandan government despite protests from Ugandans in Washington, London and South Africa.

IMPACT ON ACCESS TO FOOD

A number of civil society organisations[175] have criticized the IMF's policies for their impact on access to food, particularly in developing countries. In October 2008, former United States president Bill Clinton delivered a speech to the United Nations on World Food Day, criticizing the World Bank and IMF for their policies on food and agriculture:

We need the World Bank, the IMF, all the big foundations, and all the governments to admit that, for 30 years, we all blew it, including me when I was president. We were wrong to believe that food was like some other product in international trade, and we all have to go back to a more responsible and sustainable form of agriculture.

FORMER U.S. PRESIDENT BILL CLINTON, SPEECH AT UNITED NATIONS WORLD FOOD DAY, OCTOBER 16, 2008
The FPIF remarked that there is a recurring pattern: "the destabilization of peasant producers by a one-two punch of IMF-World Bank structural adjustment programs that gutted government investment in the countryside followed by the massive influx of subsidized U.S. and European Union agricultural imports after the WTO's Agreement on Agriculture pried open markets."

IMPACT ON PUBLIC HEALTH

A 2009 study concluded that the strict conditions resulted in thousands of deaths in Eastern Europe by tuberculosis as public health care had to be weakened. In the 21 countries to which the IMF had given loans, tuberculosis deaths rose by 16.6%. A 2017 systematic review on studies conducted on the impact that Structural adjustment programs have on child and maternal health found that these programs have a detrimental effect on maternal and child health among other adverse effects.

REFORM

The IMF is only one of many international organisations, and it is a generalist institution that deals only with macroeconomic issues; its core areas of concern in developing countries are very narrow. One proposed reform is a movement towards close partnership with other specialist agencies such as UNICEF, the Food and Agriculture Organization (FAO), and the United Nations Development Program (UNDP).

Jeffrey Sachs argues in The End of Poverty that the IMF and the World Bank have "the brightest economists and the lead in advising poor countries on how to break out of poverty, but the problem is development economics". Development economics needs the reform, not the IMF. He also notes that IMF loan conditions should be paired with other reforms—e.g., trade reform in developed nations, debt cancellation, and increased financial assistance for investments in basic infrastructure. IMF loan conditions cannot stand alone and produce change; they need to be partnered with other reforms or other conditions as applicable.

U.S. INFLUENCE AND VOTING REFORM

The scholarly consensus is that IMF decision-making is not simply technocratic, but also guided by political and economic concerns. The United States is the IMF's most powerful member, and its influence reaches even into decision-making concerning individual loan agreements. The U.S. has historically been openly opposed to losing what Treasury Secretary Jacob Lew described in 2015 as its "leadership role" at the IMF, and the U.S.' "ability to shape international norms and practices".

Emerging markets were not well-represented for most of the IMF's history: Despite being the most populous country, China's vote share was the sixth largest; Brazil's vote share was smaller than Belgium's. Reforms to give more powers to emerging economies were agreed by the G20 in 2010. The reforms could not pass, however, until they were ratified by the United States Congress, since 85% of the Fund's voting power was required for the reforms to take effect,[and the Americans held more than 16% of voting power at the time. After repeated criticism, the U.S. finally ratified the voting reforms at the end of 2015The OECD countries maintained their overwhelming majority of voting share, and the U.S. in particular retained its share at over 16%.

The criticism of the American- and European-dominated IMF has led to what some consider "disenfranchising the world" from the governance of the IMF. Raúl Prebisch, the founding secretary-general of the UN Conference on Trade and Development (UNCTAD), wrote that one of "the conspicuous deficiencies of the general economic theory, from the point of view of the periphery, is its false sense of universality".

IMF AND GLOBALIZATION

Globalization encompasses three institutions: global financial markets and transnational companies, national governments linked to each other in economic and military alliances led by the United States, and rising "global governments" such as World Trade Organization (WTO), IMF, and World Bank. Charles Derber argues in his book People Before Profit, "These interacting institutions create a new global power system where sovereignty is globalized, taking power and constitutional authority away from nations and giving it to global markets and international bodies". Titus Alexander argues that this system institutionalises global inequality between western countries and the Majority World in a form of global apartheid, in which the IMF is a key pillar.

The establishment of globalised economic institutions has been both a symptom of and a stimulus for globalisation. The development of the World Bank, the IMF, regional development banks such as the European Bank for Reconstruction and Development (EBRD), and multilateral trade institutions such as the WTO signals a move away from the dominance of the state as the primary actor analysed in international affairs. Globalization has thus been transformative in terms of limiting of state sovereignty over the economy.

INTERNATIONAL CENTRAL BANK DIGITAL CURRENCY

In April 2023, the IMF launched their international central bank digital currency through their Digital Currency Monetary Authority, it will be called the Universal Monetary Unit, or Units for shorthand. The ANSI character will be Ü and will be used to facilitate international banking and international trade between countries and currencies. It will help facilitate SWIFT transactions on cross border transactions at wholesale FX rates instantaneously with real-time settlements. In June, it announced it was working on a platform for central bank digital currencies (CBDCs) that would enable transactions between nations. IMF Managing Director Kristalina Georgieva said that if central banks did not agree on a common platform, cryptocurrencies would fill the resulting vacuum.[

SCANDALS

Managing Director Lagarde (2011–2019) was convicted of giving preferential treatment to businessman-turned-politician Bernard Tapie as he pursued a legal challenge against the French government. At the time, Lagarde was the French economic minister. Within hours of her conviction, in which she escaped any punishment, the fund's 24-member executive board put to rest any speculation that she might have to resign, praising her "outstanding leadership" and the "wide respect" she commands around the world.

Former IMF Managing Director Rodrigo Rato was arrested in 2015 for alleged fraud, embezzlement and money laundering. In 2017, the Audiencia Nacional found Rato guilty of embezzlement and sentenced him to $4+\frac{1}{2}$ years' imprisonment.[In 2018, the sentence was confirmed by the Supreme Court of Spain.

ALTERNATIVE

In March 2011, the Ministers of Economy and Finance of the African Union proposed to establish an African Monetary Fund.

At the 6th BRICS summit in July 2014 the BRICS nations (Brazil, Russia, India, China, and South Africa) announced the BRICS Contingent Reserve Arrangement (CRA) with an initial size of US$100 billion, a framework to provide liquidity through currency swaps in response to actual or potential short-term balance-of-payments pressures.

In 2014, the China-led Asian Infrastructure Investment Bank was established.

WORLD BANK (STAFF 10,000)

The World Bank is an international financial institution that provides loans and grants to the governments of low- and middle-income countries for the purpose of pursuing capital projects.[5] The World Bank is the collective name for the International Bank for Reconstruction and Development (IBRD) and International Development Association (IDA), two of five international organizations owned by the World Bank Group. It was established along with the International Monetary Fund at the 1944 Bretton Woods Conference. After a slow start, its first loan was to France in 1947. In the 1970s, it focused on loans to developing world countries, shifting away from that mission in the 1980s. For the last 30 years, it has included NGOs and environmental groups in its loan portfolio. Its loan strategy is influenced by the United Nations' Sustainable Development Goals, as well as environmental and social safeguards.

As of 2022, the World Bank is run by a president and 25 executive directors, as well as 29 various vice presidents. IBRD and IDA have 189 and 174 member countries, respectively. The U.S., Japan, China, Germany and the U.K. have the most voting power. The bank aims loans at developing countries to help reduce poverty. The bank is engaged in several global partnerships and initiatives, and takes a role in working toward addressing climate change. The World Bank operates a number of training wings, and it works with the Clean Air Initiative and the UN Development Business. It works within the Open Data Initiative and hosts an Open Knowledge Repository.

The World Bank has been criticized as promoting inflation and harming economic development, causing protests in 1988 and 2000. There has also been criticism of the bank's governance and response to the COVID-19 pandemic. The president David Malpass faced strong criticism as he challenged the scientific consensus on climate change. He was replaced by Ajay Banga, supporting climate action.

HISTORY

The World Bank was created at the 1944 Bretton Woods Conference, along with the International Monetary Fund (IMF). The president of the World Bank is traditionally an American.[9] The World Bank and the IMF are both based in Washington, D.C., and work closely with each other.

Although many countries were represented at the Bretton Woods Conference, the United States and United Kingdom were the most powerful in attendance and dominated the negotiations. The intention behind the founding of the World Bank was to provide temporary loans to low-income countries that could not obtain loans commercially. The bank may also make loans and demand policy reforms from recipients.

SOVEREIGN IMMUNITY[

The World Bank requires sovereign immunity from countries it deals with. Sovereign immunity waives a holder from all legal liability for their actions. It is proposed that this immunity from responsibility is a "shield which The World Bank wants to resort to, for escaping accountability and security by the people". As the United States has veto power, it can prevent the World Bank from taking action against its interests

OECD (STAFF 3,900)

The Organisation for Economic Co-operation and Development an inter-governmental organisation with 38 member countries, founded in 1961 to stimulate economic progress and world trade. It is a forum whose member countries describe themselves as committed to democracy and the market economy, providing a platform to compare policy experiences, seek answers to common problems, identify good practices, and coordinate domestic and international policies of its members.

The majority of OECD Members are high-income economies ranked as "very high" in the Human Development Index, and are regarded as de-veloped countries. Their collective population is 1.38 billion. As of 2017, OECD Member countries collectively comprised 62.2% of global nominal GDP (USD 49.6 trillion) and 42.8% of global GDP (Int\$54.2 trillion) at purchasing power parity. The OECD is an official United Nations observer.

In April 1948, the Organisation for European Economic Co-operation (OEEC) was established to help administer the Marshall Plan, which was rejected by both the Soviet Union and its satellite states. This would be achieved by allocating the United States' financial aid and implementing economic programs for the reconstruction of Europe after World War II. Only Western European states were members of the OEEC. Its Secretaries-General were the Frenchmen Robert Marjolin (1948–1955) and René Sergent (1955–1960). On 14 December 1960, the OEEC was reformed into the Organisation for Economic Co-operation and Development, which came into force in late September 1961, and the membership was extended to non-European states, the first of which were the United States and Canada.

The OECD's headquarters are at the Château de la Muette in Paris, France. The OECD is funded by contributions from Member countries at varying rates and had a total budget of €338.3 million in 2023, and is recognised as a highly influential publisher of mostly economic data through publications as well as annual evaluations and rankings of Member countries.

G7

The Group of Seven (G7) is an intergovernmental political and economic forum consisting of Canada, France, Germany, Italy, Japan, the United Kingdom and the United States; additionally, the European Union (EU) is a "non-enumerated member". It is organized around shared values of pluralism, liberal democracy, and representative government. G7 members are the major IMF advanced economies.

Originating from an ad hoc gathering of finance ministers in 1973, the G7 has since become a formal, high-profile venue for discussing and coordinating solutions to major global issues, especially in the areas of trade, security, economics, and climate change. Each member's head of government or state, along with the EU's Commission President and European Council President, meet annually at the G7 Summit; other high-ranking officials of the G7 and the EU meet throughout the year. Representatives of other states and international organizations are often invited as guests, with Russia having been a formal member (as part of the G8) from 1997 until its expulsion in 2014.

The G7 is not based on a treaty and has no permanent secretariat or office. It is organized through a presidency that rotates annually among the member states, with the presiding state setting the group's priorities and hosting the summit; Italy presides for 2024. While lacking a legal or institutional basis, the G7 is widely considered to wield significant international influence;[1] it has catalyzed or spearheaded several major global initiatives, including efforts to combat the HIV/AIDS pandemic, provide financial aid to developing countries, and address climate change through the 2015 Paris Agreement. However, the group has been criticized by observers for its allegedly outdated and limited membership, narrow global representation, and ineffectualness.

ACTIVITIES AND INITIATIVES

The G7 was founded primarily to facilitate shared macroeconomic initiatives in response to contemporary economic problems; the first gathering was centered around the Nixon shock, the 1970s energy crisis, and the ensuing global recession. Since 1975, the group has met annually at summits organized and hosted by whichever country occupies the annually-rotating presidency; since 1987, the G7 Finance Ministers have met at least semi-annually, and up to four times a year at stand-alone meetings.

Beginning in the 1980s, the G7 broadened its areas of concern to include issues of international security, human rights, and global security; for example, during this period, the G7 concerned itself with the ongoing Iran-Iraq War and Soviet occupation of Afghanistan. In the 1990s, it launched a debt-relief program for the 42 heavily indebted poor countries (HIPC);[50] provided $300 million to help build the Shelter Structure over the damaged reactor at Chernobyl;[j] and established the Financial Stability Forum to help in "managing the international monetary system".

At the turn of the 21st century, the G7 began emphasizing engagement with the developing world. At the 1999 summit, the group helped launch the G20, a similar forum made up of the G7 and the next 13 largest economies (including the European Union), in order to "promote dialogue between major industrial and emerging market countries"; the G20 has been touted by some of its members as a replacement for the G7. Having previously announced a plan to cancel 90% of bilateral debt for the HIPC, totaling $100 billion, in 2005 the G7 announced debt reductions of "up to 100%" to be negotiated on a "case by case" basis.

Following the global financial crisis of 2007–2008, which was the worst of its kind since 1970s, the G7 met twice in Washington, D.C. in 2008 and in Rome, the following February. News media reported that much of the world was looking to the group for leadership and solutions. G7 finance ministers pledged to take "all necessary steps" to stem the crisis, devising an "aggressive action plan" that included providing publicly funded capital infusions to banks in danger of failing. Some analysts criticized the group for seemingly advocating that individual governments develop individual responses to the recession, rather than cohere around a united effort.

In subsequent years, the G7 has faced several geopolitical challenges that have led some international analysts to question its credibility, or propose its replacement by the G20. On 2 March 2014, the G7 condemned the Russian Federation for its "violation of the sovereignty and territorial integrity of Ukraine" through its military intervention. The group also announced its commitment to "mobilize rapid technical assistance to support Ukraine in addressing its macroeconomic, regulatory and anti-corruption challenges", while adding that the International Monetary Fund (IMF) was best suited to stabilizing the country's finances and economy.

HOST VENUES OF G7 SUMMITS IN JAPAN

In response to Russia's subsequent annexation of Crimea, on 24 March the G7 convened an emergency meeting at the official residence of the Prime Minister of the Netherlands, the Catshuis in The Hague; this location was chosen because all G7 leaders were already present to attend the 2014 Nuclear Security Summit hosted by the Netherlands. This was the first G7 meeting neither taking place in a member state nor having the host leader participating in the meeting. The upcoming G8 summit in Sochi, Russia was moved to Brussels, where the EU was the host. On 5 June 2014 the G7 condemned Moscow for its "continuing violation" of Ukraine's sovereignty and stated they were prepared to impose further sanctions on Russia.[66] This meeting was the first since Russia was suspended from the G8, and subsequently it has not been involved in any G7 summit.

The G7 has continued to take a strong stance against Russia's "destabilising behaviour and malign activities" in Ukraine and elsewhere around the world, following the joint communique from the June 2021 summit in the U.K. The group also called on Russia to address international cybercrime attacks launched from within its borders, and to investigate the use of chemical weapons on Russian opposition leader Alexei Navalny.[67] The June 2021 summit also saw the G7 commit to helping the world recover from the global COVID-19 pandemic (including plans to help vaccinate the entire world); encourage further action against climate change and biodiversity loss; and promote "shared values" of pluralism and democracy.[35]

G20

The G20 or Group of 20 is an intergovernmental forum comprising 19 sovereign countries, the European Union (EU), and the African Union (AU). It works to address major issues related to the global economy, such as international financial stability, climate change mitigation and sustainable development.

The G20 is composed of most of the world's largest economies' finance ministries, including both industrialised and developing countries; it accounts for around 80% of gross world product (GWP), 75% of international trade, two-thirds of the global population, and 60% of the world's land area.

The G20 was founded in 1999 in response to several world economic crises.[8] Since 2008, it has convened at least once a year, with summits involving each member's head of government or state, finance minister, or foreign minister, and other high-ranking officials; the EU is represented by the European Commission and the European Central Bank. Other countries, international organizations, and nongovernmental organizations are invited to attend the summits, some permanently. In 2023, during its 2023 summit, the African Union joined as its 21st member.

In its 2009 summit, the G20 declared itself the primary venue for international economic and financial cooperation. The group's stature has risen during the subsequent decade, and it is recognised by analysts as exercising considerable global influence; it is also criticized for its limited membership, lack of enforcement powers, and for the alleged undermining of existing international institutions. Summits are often met with protests, particularly by anti-globalization groups.

MEMBERS

As of 2023, there are 21 members in the group: Argentina, Australia, Brazil, Canada, China, France, Germany, India, Indonesia, Italy, Japan, Mexico, Russia, Saudi Arabia, South Africa, South Korea, Turkey, the United Kingdom, the United States, the European Union and the African Union. Guest invitees include, amongst others, Spain, the United Nations, the World Bank and ASEAN.

LDC (LEAST DEVELOPED COUNTRIES)

The least developed countries (LDCs) are developing countries listed by the United Nations that exhibit the lowest indicators of socioeconomic development. The concept of LDCs originated in the late 1960s and the first group of LDCs was listed by the UN in its resolution 2768 (XXVI) on 18 November 1971.

A country is classified among the Least Developed Countries if it meets three criteria:

- Poverty – adjustable criterion based on Gross national income (GNI) per capita averaged over three years. As of 2018, a country must have GNI per capita less than US$1,025 to be included on the list, and over $1,230 to graduate from it.
- Human resource weakness (based on indicators of nutrition, health, education and adult literacy).
- Economic vulnerability (based on instability of agricultural production, instability of exports of goods and services, economic importance of non-traditional activities, merchandise export concentration, handicap of economic smallness, and the percentage of population displaced by natural disasters).

As of December 2023, 45 countries were still classified as LDC, while seven graduated between 1994 and 2023. The World Trade Organization (WTO) recognizes the UN list and says that "Measures taken in the framework of the WTO can help LDCs increase their exports to other WTO members and attract investment. In many developing countries, pro-market reforms have encouraged faster growth, diversification of exports, and more effective participation in the multilateral trading system."

The following 45 countries were still listed as least developed countries by the UN as of December 2023: Afghanistan, Angola, Bangladesh, Benin, Burkina Faso, Burundi, Cambodia, Central African Republic, Chad, Comoros, Democratic Republic of Congo, Djibouti, Eritrea, Ethiopia, Gambia, Guinea, Guinea-Bissau, Haiti, Kiribati, Laos, Lesotho, Liberia, Madagascar, Malawi, Mali, Mauritania, Mozambique, Myanmar, Nepal, Niger, Rwanda, São Tomé and Príncipe, Senegal, Sierra Leone, Solomon

Islands, Somalia, South Sudan, Sudan, East Timor, Togo, Tuvalu, Uganda, Tanzania, Yemen, Zambia.

BY CONTINENT OR REGION

There are 33 countries that are classified as least developed countries in Africa, eight in Asia, three in Oceania, and one in the Americas.

MODERN SLAVERY (poverty reduction and crime reduction will have a dramatic positive impact)

> According to the latest Global Estimates of Modern Slavery (2022) from Walk Free, the International Labor Organization and the International Organization for Migration: 49.6 million people live in modern slavery – in forced labor and forced marriage.

Who has highest rate of slavery in the world?

North Korea, Eritrea and Burundi are estimated to have the world's highest rates of modern-day slavery, with India, China and Pakistan home to the largest number of victims. Jul 30, 2018

Is there more slavery today than ever?

> Experts have calculated that roughly 13 million people were captured and sold as slaves between the 15th and 19th centuries; today, an estimated 40.3 million people – more than three times the figure during the transatlantic slave trade – are living in some form of modern slavery, according to the latest figures. Feb 25, 2019

TOP TEN LIST OF GLOBAL SPORTS ORGANISATIONS (REDUCE LEVEL OF EARNINGS TO FACILITATE WIDER AFFORDABLE TICKET PRICES/ EARNINGS IN THE FILM AND TV INDUSTRIES TO BE SCALED BACK)

This list of the top 10 most popular sports from around the world is based on data collected by Michael Brown of biggestglobalsports.com, using the amount of coverage from major online sports news websites, with the amount of coverage weighted by country size (using 50/50 weighting for population and wealth).

This data is part of the <u>Topend sports analysis</u> of the world's most popular sport.

RANK	SPORT	INDEX
1.	Soccer / Association Football	3001
2.	Basketball	1394
3.	Tennis	1170
4.	Cricket	914
5.	F1	557
6.	Baseball	552
7.	Athletics	500
8.	American Football	449
9.	Boxing	446
10.	Golf	426

How big is the global sports sponsorship market?

> Sponsorships are a significant source of revenue for franchises operating within the sports industry. In 2022, the global sports sponsorship market was worth an estimated 66 billion U.S. dollars and was expected to grow to almost 108 billion U.S. dollars by 2030. Jan 10, 2024
>
> The global value of sports media rights has increased to a record high of almost $56bn (€51.1bn/£44.7bn), SportsBusiness' Global Media Report 2023 reveals. Nov 27, 2023
>
> The global sports events tickets market size was estimated at USD 15.47 billion in 2022 expected to reach USD 19.26 billion in 2023.

Database finding:

1) Player: Tiger Woods (Golf, 2009)

Average weekly salary per player: **£128,429** ($210,540)

2) New York Yankees: No1 payers, regular season WL: 103-59. World Series winners. (Baseball, 2009)

Average weekly salary per player: **£89,897** ($147,372)

3) Dallas Mavericks: No1 payers, regular season WL: 50-32. Conf S-F. (Basketball, 2008-09)

Average weekly salary per player: **£68,343** ($112,037)

4) Royal Challengers Bangalore: No1 payers, finished IPL runners-up. (Cricket, 2009)

Average weekly salary per player: **£57,833** ($94,808)

5) Manchester United: finished 1st in EPL. (Football, 2008-09)

Average weekly salary per player: **£57,072** ($93,561)

6) Dallas Cowboys: No1 payers, WLT 9-7-0, no post-season. (American football, 2008-09)

Average weekly salary per player: **£32,404** ($53,121)

FILM AND ENTERTAINMENT (SCALE BACK EARNINGS)

The annual revenue of the global film industry as of 2022 was $77 billion. The top countries by the market by the year 2025 in terms of projected highest revenue are China and the United States of America. The world-wide cinema box office revenue as of 2022 was $26 billion as stated by film industry statistics.

Information sources: *Wikipedia, Economist, USA stats, United Nations, US News, World Report, Global Database of Humanitarian, Organisations, Pen Reserve Center, Ericsson, World Bank, World Health Organisation, Stephen Poole (Guardian 2017), Randall W Stone, Economist, William Easterly, Jeffery Sachs, Jeremy Garlick, Eric Toussaint, Dennis Millet, Joseph E. Stiglitz, Ermwin Blumenthal, Bill Clinton ,Jacob Lew, Ron Prebisch, Walk Free, Sport Busines Global Metro Report, Charities Aid Foundation Giving Index.*

Manufactured by Amazon.ca
Bolton, ON